A
SCRAP
OF
TIME

IDA
FINK

A
SCRAP
OF
TIME
AND OTHER STORIES

**TRANSLATED FROM THE POLISH
BY MADELINE LEVINE
AND FRANCINE PROSE**

NORTHWESTERN UNIVERSITY PRESS

EVANSTON, ILLINOIS

Northwestern University Press
Evanston, Illinois 60208-4210

Originally published in the Polish language as *Skrawek Czasu* by Aneks
Publishers, London. Copyright © 1983 by Ida Fink. English translation
first published by Pantheon Books, a division of Random House Inc., in
1987; copyright © by Random House Inc. Northwestern University Press
edition published 1995 by arrangement with Ida Fink. All rights reserved.

The story "A Scrap of Time" first appeared in *The New Yorker*.

Printed in the United States of America

ISBN 0-8101-1259-0

Second paperback printing 1996
Third paperback printing 1997

Library of Congress Cataloging-in-Publication Data

Fink, Ida.
      [Scrawek czasu. English]
      A scrap of time and other stories / Ida Fink ; translated from the
Polish by Madeline Levine and Francine Prose.
            p.   cm. — (Jewish lives)
      Originally published: New York : Pantheon Books, 1987.
      ISBN 0-8101-1259-0 (paper : alk. paper)
      1. Holocaust, Jewish (1939–1945)—Fiction. 2. Poland—Social life
and customs—Fiction. I. Title. II. Series.
PG7165.I44S513 1995
891.8′537—dc20   95-15281
                                                              CIP

The paper in this publication meets the minimum requirements of the
American National Standard for Information Sciences—Permanence of
Paper for Printed Library Materials, ANSI Z.39.48-1984.

102997-1905X8

For Bronek

CONTENTS

A
SCRAP
OF
TIME

A
SCRAP
OF
TIME

I want to talk about a certain time not measured in months and years. For so long I have wanted to talk about this time, and not in the way I will talk about it now, not just about this one scrap of time. I wanted to, but I couldn't, I didn't know how. I was afraid, too, that this second time, which is measured in months and years, had buried the other time under a layer of years, that this second time had crushed the first and destroyed it within me. But no. Today, digging around in the ruins of memory, I found it fresh and untouched by forgetfulness. This time was measured not in months but in a word—we no longer said "in the beautiful month of May," but "after the first 'action,' or the second, or right before the third." We had different measures of time, we different ones, always different, always with that mark of difference that moved some of us to pride and others to humility. We, who because of our difference were condemned once again, as we had been before in our history, we were condemned once again during this time measured not in months nor by the rising and setting of the sun, but by a word—"action," a word signifying movement, a word you would use about a novel or a play.

I don't know who used the word first, those who acted or those who were the victims of their action; I don't know who created this technical term, who substituted it for the first term, "round-up"—a word that became devalued (or dignified?) as time passed, as new methods were developed, and "round-up" was distinguished from "action" by the borderline of race. Round-ups were for forced labor.

We called the first action—that scrap of time that I want to talk about—a round-up, although no one was rounding anyone up; on that beautiful, clear morning, each of us made our way, not willingly, to be sure, but under orders, to the marketplace in our little town, a rectangle enclosed by high, crooked buildings—a pharmacy, clothing stores, an ironmonger's shop—and framed by a sidewalk made of big square slabs that time had fractured and broken. I have never again seen such huge slabs. In the middle of the marketplace stood the town hall, and it was right there, in front of the town hall, that we were ordered to form ranks.

I should not have written "we," for I was not standing in the ranks, although, obeying the order that had been posted the previous evening, I had left my house after eating a perfectly normal breakfast, at a table that was set in a normal way, in a room whose doors opened onto a garden veiled in morning mists, dry and golden in the rising sun.

Our transformation was not yet complete; we were still living out of habit in that old time that was measured in months and years, and on that lovely peaceful morning, filled with dry, golden mists, we took the words "conscription of labor" literally, and as mature people tend to read between the lines, our imaginations replaced the word "labor" with "labor camp," one of which, people said, was being built nearby. Apparently those who gave the order were perfectly aware of the poverty of our imaginations; that is why they saved themselves work by issuing a written order. This is how accurately they predicted our responses: after finishing a normal breakfast, at a normally set table, the older members of the family decided to disobey the order because they were afraid of the heavy physical labor, but they did not advise the young to do likewise—the young, who, if their disobedience were discovered, would not be able to plead old age. We were like infants.

This beautiful, clear morning that I am digging out of the ruins of my memory is still fresh; its colors and aromas have not faded: a grainy golden mist with red spheres of apples hanging in it, and the shadows above the river damp with the sharp odor of burdock, and the bright blue dress that I was wearing when I left the house and when I turned around at the gate. It was then, probably at that very moment, that I suddenly progressed, instinctively, from an infantile state to a still naive caution—instinctively, because I wasn't thinking about why I avoided the gate that led to the street and instead set off on a roundabout route, across the orchard, along the riverbank, down a road we called "the back way" because it wound through the outskirts of town. Instinctively, because at that moment I still did not know that I wouldn't stand in the marketplace in front of the town hall. Perhaps I wanted to delay that moment, or perhaps I simply liked the river.

Along the way, I stopped and carefully picked out flat stones, and skipped them across the water; I sat down for a while on the little bridge, beyond which one could see the town, and dangled my legs, looking at my reflection in the water and at the willows that grew on the bank. I was not yet afraid then, nor was my sister. (I forgot to say that my younger sister was with me, and she, too, skipped stones across the water and dangled her legs over the river, which is called the Gniezna—a pitiful little stream, some eight meters wide.) My sister, too, was not yet afraid; it was only when we went further along the street, beyond the bridge, and the view of the marketplace leapt out at us from behind the building on the corner, that we suddenly stopped in our tracks.

There was the square, thick with people as on a market day, only different, because a market-day crowd is colorful and loud, with chickens clucking, geese honking, and people talking and bargaining. This crowd was silent. In a way it resembled a rally—but it was different from that, too. I don't know what it was exactly. I only know that we suddenly stopped and my sister began to tremble, and then I caught the trembling, and she said, "Let's run away," and although no one was chasing us and the morning was still clear and peaceful, we ran back to the little bridge, but we no longer noticed the willows or the reflections of our running figures in the water; we ran for a long time until we were high up the steep slope known as Castle Hill—the ruins of an old castle stood on top of it—and on this hillside, the jewel of our town, we sat down in the bushes, out of breath and still shaking.

From this spot we could see our house and our garden—it was just as it always was, nothing had changed—and we could see our neighbor's house, from which our neighbor had emerged, ready to beat her carpets. We could hear the slap slap of her carpet beater.

We sat there for an hour, maybe two, I don't know, because it was then that time measured in the ordinary way stopped. Then we climbed down the steep slope to the river and returned to our house, where we heard what had happened in the marketplace, and that our cousin David had been taken, and how they took him, and what message he had left for his mother. After they were taken away, he wrote down again what he had asked people to tell her; he threw a note out of the truck and a peasant brought it to her that evening—but that happened later. First we learned that the women had been told to go home, that only the men were ordered to remain standing there, and that the path chosen by our cousin had been the opposite of ours. We had been horrified by the sight of the crowd in the marketplace, while he was drawn towards it by an enormous force, a force as strong as his nerves were weak, so that somehow or other he did violence to his own fate, he himself, himself, himself, and that was what he asked people to tell his mother, and then he wrote it down: "I myself am to blame, forgive me."

We would never have guessed that he belonged to the race of the Impatient Ones, doomed to destruction by their anxiety and their inability to remain still, never—because he was round-faced and chubby, not at all energetic, the sort of person who can't be pulled away from his book, who smiles timidly, girlishly. Only the end of the war brought us the truth about his last hours. The peasant who delivered the note did not dare to tell us what he saw, and although other people, too, muttered something about what they had seen, no one dared to believe it, especially since the Germans offered proofs of another truth that each of us grasped at greedily; they measured out doses of it sparingly, with restraint—a perfect cover-up. They went to such trouble, created so many phantoms, that only time, time measured not in months and years, opened our eyes and convinced us.

Our cousin David had left the house later than we did,

and when he reached the marketplace it was already known
—not by everyone, to be sure, but by the so-called Council,
which in time became the *Judenrat*—that the words "conscription for labor" had nothing to do with a labor camp.
One friend, a far-sighted older man, ordered the boy to hide
just in case, and since it was too late to return home
because the streets were blocked off, he led him to his own
apartment in one of the houses facing the marketplace.
Like us, not comprehending that the boy belonged to the
race of the Impatient Ones, who find it difficult to cope
with isolation and who act on impulse, he left David in a
room that locked from inside. What our cousin experienced,
locked up in that room, will remain forever a mystery.
Much can be explained by the fact that the room had a
view of the marketplace, of that silent crowd, of the faces
of friends and relatives, and it may be that finally the isolation of his hiding place seemed to him more unbearable
than the great and threatening unknown outside the
window—an unknown shared by all who were gathered in
the marketplace.

It was probably a thought that came in a flash: not to be
alone, to be together with everyone. All that was needed
was one movement of his hand.

I think it incorrect to assume that he left the hiding
place because he was afraid that they would search the
houses. That impatience of the heart, that trembling of the
nerves, the burden of isolation, condemned him to extermi-
nation together with the first victims of our town.

He stood between a lawyer's apprentice and a student of
architecture and to the question, "Profession?" he replied,
"Teacher," although he had been a teacher for only a short

time and quite by chance. His neighbor on the right also told the truth, but the architecture student lied, declaring himself a carpenter, and this lie saved his life—or, to be more precise, postponed the sentence of death for two years.

Seventy people were loaded into trucks; at the last moment the rabbi was dragged out of his house—he was the seventy-first. On the way to the trucks they marched past the ranks of all those who had not yet managed to inform the interrogators about the work they did. It was then that our cousin said out loud, "Tell my mother that it's my own fault and that I beg her forgiveness." Presumably, he had already stopped believing what all of us still believed later: that they were going to a camp. He had that horrifying clarity of vision that comes just before death.

The peasant who that evening brought us the note that said, "I myself am to blame, forgive me," was somber and didn't look us in the eye. He said he had found the note on the road to Lubianki and that he didn't know anything else about it; we knew that he knew, but we did not want to admit it. He left, but he came back after the war to tell us what he had seen.

A postcard from the rabbi arrived two days later, convincing everyone that those who had been taken away were in a labor camp. A month later, when the lack of any further news began to make us doubt the camp, another postcard arrived, this one written by someone else who had been deported—an accountant, I think. After the postcard scheme came the payment of contributions: the authorities let it be understood that kilos of coffee or tea—or gold—would provide a family with news of their dear ones. As a gesture of compassion they also allowed people to send food parcels to the prisoners, who, it was said, were working in a camp in the Reich. Once again, after the second action, a postcard turned up. It was written in pencil and almost indecipherable. After this postcard, we said, "They're done for." But rumors told a different story altogether—of soggy earth in the woods by the village of Lubianki, and of a bloodstained handkerchief that had been found. These rumors came from nowhere; no eyewitnesses stepped forward.

The peasant who had not dared to speak at the time came back after the war and told us everything. It happened just as rumor had it, in a dense, overgrown forest, eight kilometers outside of town, one hour after the trucks left the marketplace. The execution itself did not take long; more time was spent on the preparatory digging of the grave.

At the first shots, our chubby, round-faced cousin David, who was always clumsy at gymnastics and sports, climbed a tree and wrapped his arms around the trunk like a child hugging his mother, and that was the way he died.

THE GARDEN THAT FLOATED AWAY

Once I saw a garden float away. It was our neighbors' garden, just as beautiful and lush as ours, and there were fruit trees growing in it, just as in ours. I saw it float away, slowly and majestically, into the distance far beyond our reach.

That afternoon was warm and peaceful. I was sitting with my sister on the porch steps, and the two gardens—Wojciech's and ours—were right there in front of our eyes. They formed a single garden, for they were not divided by a fence. A fence, we said, would be an intrusion. Only a row of evenly spaced currant bushes stitched the two gardens together.

It was a peaceful afternoon. The sun was lazy and golden. Wojciech stepped onto his porch—the houses, too, were twins—and called to us, "Let's go pick the russet apples."

We used to do the chores in both gardens at the same

time: we mowed the grass on the same day, painted the tree trunks white on the same day, and so, out of habit, he told us about the apple picking.

Right after he shouted we saw Wojciech's elder sister. She was carrying two large wicker baskets, just like the one we had in our attic. Wojciech's sister didn't say anything to us. She just went into the garden, placed her baskets under the largest golden russet, and returned to the yard for a ladder.

"Wojciech," she yelled, "get the newspapers ready!"

Every single apple first has to be gently and carefully plucked from the branch, then gently and carefully wrapped in paper to keep it from freezing over the winter, then gently and carefully placed in a wicker basket, and finally, up in the attic, they all have to be gently and carefully lifted out of the basket and set on the floor one by one, next to, but not touching, each other. This gentle carefulness, or careful gentleness, is essential in handling fruit.

Wojciech disappeared from the porch and returned a moment later with a stack of newspapers under his arm. And once more he shouted to us, "We're picking the russets!"

We were sitting on the porch steps, waiting for Father to finish talking with Mrs. Kasinska and call us in. Their conversation was taking place in his office, which was dusty and unused now, though sometimes a patient still appeared in the evening under cover of darkness with a loaf of black bread in his basket as payment. From time to time we could hear Mrs. Kasinska's animated voice, but we couldn't hear Father at all. They had been talking for a long time.

Wojciech climbed up the ladder; his sister stood under the tree and raised her arms, as if she were getting ready to dance the *kujawiak* or some other country dance. She would take the fruit that Wojciech picked and bend down over the basket, then straighten up and raise her arms again. I watched every movement of this fruit-gathering dance, so gentle and full of tenderness. We only wanted to watch, not to eavesdrop, but we couldn't help overhearing. True, they were speaking softly and not every word reached us, but sometimes you only have to hear a few words to know what someone is saying.

"Bare," they said. "Green."

"They are right," they said.

"What will happen in the winter?" they said.

They were saying that we had eaten up all our fruit while it was still green, and that we were right to do so, because who knows what would happen to us by winter. What they were saying was absolutely true.

I watched so attentively that my eyes began to hurt from watching. The sun ignited little fires on the masts of the trees. How could I have known that this was the signal to set sail?

Wojciech's garden, the garden of our childhood friend, suddenly shuddered, swayed, began to pitch and roll, and slowly, slowly, it started to float away, like a huge green ocean liner. It sailed away slowly but steadily; the distance between us grew quickly, the garden got smaller and disappeared. It had floated away to an inaccessible distance, far beyond our reach.

I felt confused and unhappy, because all through my childhood it had been close by. I don't know what would have happened next if my sister hadn't said, "Don't squint like that. When you squint anyone can see right away that you're Jewish."

As soon as she said that, everything suddenly returned to its place—the garden and the trees, the baskets and the ladder, Wojciech and his sister. But who could believe in such a return? Not me.

Father called us to his office, to the animated Mrs. Kasinska, who, once the price was agreed on, promised to make *Kennkarten* for us so we could be saved, so we would not be killed.

BEHIND THE HEDGE

Agafia stands in the doorway, leaning against the wall. She is short and sturdy with a shiny face; her eyes—small, shapeless, dark brown, filmed with a constant mist of tears—look like marinated mushrooms. Sometimes those mushrooms make me laugh, sometimes they infuriate me. It depends on Agafia's mood, not mine. Agafia announces her moods by slamming doors, by banging pots, and also by the flashes of light in her small shapeless eyes. Right now, I would like her to lower the windowshades—it's a stuffy day in July—but I don't say anything. I know that Agafia is preparing for one of her stories, which she has told me nearly every day for almost twenty years, and which, if they were written down, would make up a chronicle of our little town and its inhabitants. These stories are very complex, although they are about simple matters, and are full of tiny details that at first seem extraneous but which by the end turn out to be what make the stories vivid and complete.

Agafia's stories are my only link to the outside world. For years I have not left my chair, to which I am confined by the weakness in my legs. I see no one, and the muffled, distant echoes of daily life reach me across the high, thick hedge that my husband planted long ago.

Nonetheless, for a year now, that is to say, since we fell victim of the *Herrenvolk* and life began to abound with unheard-of cruelties, Agafia's reports have become my only way of participating—emotionally, passively—in the history of our days. I should also note that it was thanks to Agafia that my house—a spacious, one-family house, situated in an orchard of seventy-eight fruit trees—escaped being requisitioned as living quarters for German officers. To this day I do not know how she managed that. When I asked, she answered evasively, "Those bastards, I won't give them a goddamn thing, no lodging for them!" A few days later, when I discovered that my Rosenthal china was missing, it occurred to me that she had cunningly bribed them, especially since when I asked Agafia about it directly she flew into a rage. "People have nothing to eat and all you think about is your Rosenthals! Pfoo!" I fell silent, ashamed of myself. She was absolutely right.

The sun is broiling hot. A reddish haze of dust, shimmering in the rays of sun, rises from the heavy brocade drapes and from the carpets, which have not been beaten in a long time. Agafia's silence continues. She has a dingy cloth tied around her waist instead of an apron and is standing in the doorway—she always tells her stories standing up—with an empty tray in her hands. This time I foresee a symphony, an epic, and with great effort I get out of my chair and inch across the carpet towards the window to block out the sun. One pull on the cord obliterates the bright spot of green and the abundant sunflowers, gracefully bending towards the south; it silences the buzzing of the bees, shields me from the aroma of the hot grass. A sudden darkness the color of heavy red wine descends on the room. I struggle all the way

back to my chair and wait for her usual coarse comment—
"It won't hurt you. Exercise is good for you." But Agafia
isn't even looking at me; I can see that she is considering
the first words she will say as soon as I sit down again in
my worn chair. I sit facing the door, I raise my head slightly,
I am ready.

"Today they shot two truckloads of Jews in the pasture,"
Agafia begins, and looks me straight in the eye with her
teary mushroom gaze. Automatically I lift my hands to my
temples, but I let them drop instantly, rebuked by her
sharp gaze.

"We have to know." I remember her words when she first
told me about the horrors the Nazis were committing in our
town, and I protested weakly, "Agafia, dear, I can't listen
to that, I'm sick. Spare me."

"We have to know about it. And look at it. And remember," she replied, and after that I didn't dare interrupt her.

"They shot them in the morning; you were still asleep. I
woke up early; my brother and I were going to Lubianki for
some flour. There wasn't a bit of flour in the pantry! When
we got there it was seven o'clock. Mikolaj buried the sack
in the straw, and, though they offered us milk, we didn't
stop to drink any. We figured, it's time to go back, why
show ourselves to the Germans in daylight? Also, it's nice
to travel in the morning—it's cool out, birds are chattering
in the woods, the grass has dew on it, the white mist on the
fields looks just like flowering buckwheat. Mikolaj and I
got to talking about the old days when he was courting the
miller's daughter who married somebody else. Just remem-
bering it, Mikolaj almost died laughing. That mist on the
fields, it covered the world. When we came out of the
woods, we still couldn't see anything. The horse pricked up
his ears; something was making him nervous. You see, the

horse was the first to figure out that something awful was happening. But not us—not till we heard the first shot. Very close. The gray reared up. Mikolaj pulled on the reins and jumped down from the wagon. We were right on the road. What could we do? We heard voices—we couldn't tell if they were far or near—it was as if the fog had stuffed cotton into our ears. Every couple of minutes there was a shot, a little bit of screaming, and then silence. I got all soaked with sweat, especially here, between my breasts; my blouse was sticking to me like after a bath. 'Don't be scared,' Mikolaj said. 'They're shooting the Jews. Get down from the wagon and go into the woods. We can't drive past there now. We have to wait till they finish.' He turned the wagon around, slowly, quiet as can be, parked it in a hazel grove beside the road. Meanwhile the fog had lifted, so when I sat down on the grass at the edge of the woods, I could see everything, every single blessed thing . . ."

Agafia must have seen how pale I was, for she stopped and gave me an ironic look as I reached for a glass of tea. A bit of sugar sifted off the teaspoon; my hand was trembling.

"If I told people what a sensitive thing you are, they would laugh. Nowadays you have to have a tough tenderness. Tough. Any other kind isn't worth shit."

Agafia's marinated mushrooms glittered sternly. I put down the glass.

"There weren't very many of them—seventy people at most and a handful of Germans. They took them at night, in the outskirts, from that neighborhood near the pond. They're taking them pretty often now, to make sure that everyone left fits into the ghetto. The Germans walked up and down, with their guns loaded, and whenever one of them shouted, it was like barking dogs. The Jews were digging trenches, some of them were already lying on the ground. They dug quietly, seriously, not just any which way. Think about it—digging your own grave. What did they feel while they were digging? Do you know?"

I shook my head.

"But *I* know! *Nothing*, thank you. They didn't feel anything anymore. They were dead before they died. When they started shooting again, I jumped up and wanted to run into the woods, so I wouldn't have to see. But I didn't run. Something kept me there and said to me: 'Watch. Don't shut your eyes.' So I watched."

Agafia was silent. I sat motionless, feeling my helplessness more than ever before, the burden of being crippled. Agafia put down the tray, unpinned the cloth from her waist, and wiped her face. She came closer, pulled up a chair. Her sitting down was unusual and it terrified me.

"Do you know who was there with them?" she asked in a hushed voice, staring at me. "That young dark-haired girl, the one you chased away . . ."

I asked sharply, "And how do *you* know that, Agafia? *You* didn't see her!"

"I know."

And I knew that she was telling the truth.

"Didn't you say that she was pretty as a picture, with black hair and long braids? I know. I even know whose daughter she was."

She looked at me and I felt faint. I wanted to tell her to stop looking at me, that one thing has nothing to do with the other, but I couldn't speak. I moved my lips soundlessly and withdrew into myself. Suddenly I smelled flowers, I saw the pale, delicate face of the fifteen-year-old girl.

"Am I saying you're guilty of her death?" asked Agafia, who could read one's thoughts.

"I'm not guilty of anything!" I wanted to scream, but now, though I felt able to speak, I realized that I could not honestly say those words. And Agafia knew that I knew.

She stood up. Her short, sturdy figure seemed suddenly dignified and regal. She pinned the cloth around her waist again and picked up the tray and the plates from the table. In the doorway she turned around.

"She was standing there naked in the empty pasture, with the sun shining on her, waiting for them to kill her. But the one who was aiming at her couldn't shoot. He must have had an eye for beauty. He stood there and took aim, and she stood there and waited. Then another one of them ran up to him, a blond man, and shouted something in their language. He shoved the first one out of the way and fired the gun himself. She waved her little hands in the air, fell down, and lay still."

In the long silence that followed, we exchanged glances, Agafia and I. After a while I lowered my gaze and she left the room, slamming the door. The next sound that reached me was the noisy, metallic banging of pots being put away.

The hardest part is when I start to move. Then, when I feel the support of my cane, the effort of lifting my legs diminishes my sense of helplessness. After twenty years I have grown used to being crippled, just as I have grown used to Agafia's constant presence and to the isolation I sank into when my husband left me. Sometimes it even seems to me that the life I have spent inside the four walls of my house and the four green walls of my beautiful garden is a happy life. Step by step I hobble across the room in which the darkness, the color of wine—or of blood—is deeper; the sun has already moved from the south to the west. My rubber-tipped cane makes a dull sound. With my other hand I touch each piece of furniture, one by one: the oak table, the broad oak credenza, the bookcase. I walk slowly, deliberately, though common sense tells me not to move. I walk, obeying perhaps the gaze of Agafia, who can still make me feel a sickly child's fear.

Bright light, bursting through the open door, hurts my eyes. The orchard is silent; the bees, so noisy at midday, have grown quiet; there is only the sound of crickets and the chirping of the sparrows stripping the cherries from the trees. The sunflowers have turned their heads towards the sun, which is already going down. For me this is the most beautiful moment. I can't bear early mornings with their promise of full bloom, nor midday, priding itself on its gorgeous beauty. But sunset, slowly but inevitably descending into night, awakens in me neither anxiety nor sorrow.

A path bordered by currant bushes leads me to my destination. It was right here, among flowers that were once laid out in formal beds but now grow wild in a tangled mass, that I saw that girl, that child. She was lying on the ground half naked; her beauty went straight to my heart. Frail, delicate—only when she raised her eyes did I realize: a child.

"Shame on you!" I screamed at her. "For shame! At your age! In someone else's garden . . . Get out of here! Immediately!"

I didn't look at the boy, only at her. She got up from the ground and hastily, embarrassed, covered her nakedness.

"We're sorry," she whispered.

Her eyes were still warm with love, and her movements had a sensual heaviness that was strange and unnatural for her girlish body. They were beginning to walk away, but I kept on screaming about how rotten and debauched our young people were becoming.

"For shame," I repeated. "At your age . . . Shame on you!"

The more I shouted the colder and angrier the girl's eyes became. I thought she was going to strike me. But she spoke quietly, bitterly.

"We're not allowed to do anything. We're not even allowed to love each other, or make each other happy. All we're allowed to do is die. 'At your age,' you say. And will we get any older? Come on, Zygmunt," she turned to the boy, "let's get out of here."

They left by the same path that I had come on a moment earlier. The boy said, "Ssh. She's a jealous old woman, she's a cripple. Ssh . . ." And I realized that she was crying.

I watched them until they disappeared, expelled from paradise. Then I looked sadly at the broken flowers, the crushed grass. And I thought about how I hadn't even seen the boy. I know that there was a boy with her and he was named Zygmunt. But I didn't see him.

Now the flowers here grow straight, untouched. Theirs were the last feet that touched this grass. What am I looking for as I bend down towards the ground? That moment of love and happiness, which they tried greedily to save from their broken life? That I stole from them? What words are my lips whispering? She waved her little hands in the air, fell down, and lay still . . .

How fortunate it is that Agafia, who always knows when she's needed, is coming now. She walks briskly towards me, and her face is kindly, but still stern. Now she is beside me; I feel her hand grasping my arm.

"All right, all right," she says.

We walk back in silence. The only sound that can be heard is our breathing and the crunch of gravel on the path.

* * * * *

Hidden in the dark interiors of apartments, with our faces
pressed against windowpanes damp from rain and from our
rapid breaths, we, reprieved until the next time, looked out
at the condemned, who stood in the marketplace, in the
same spot where on fair days the cheerful town erects its
stalls. Divided into groups of four, they were waiting for
the command to set out. And the rain kept falling—it
didn't stop for one minute that night, a night that those
who survived will remember as the Night of the Old Men.
Because those who stood in those groups of four were old,
worn out with work, and many of them probably had
trouble walking to their destination, which was the green
ravine near the railroad station where our children—their
grandchildren—used to go sledding. We also looked at the
six SS-men. In the long capes that shielded them from the
rain, in their high, shiny boots, they strutted around,
spattering mud on the old men, and one of them, the
youngest, kept running to the far end of the marketplace,
where he would stand in the doorway of the pharmacy and
watch for something. That watching made us anxious; and
there was also a growing impatience in the faces of the SS.
Only the old people waiting for the command to set out
remained unconcerned. Finally, when the young SS-man
had run to the pharmacy entrance for the fourth time and,
cheerful now, shouted out something we didn't understand,
but that was clearly good news, we saw the truck approach-

ing the marketplace with shovels in the back. We also saw the young SS-man strike the driver in the face, while the others formed a black ring, encircling the groups of four. It was then—the old men of our town were already on their way and were passing their homes and the children and grandchildren hidden behind their windows—it was then that the door of one of those houses opened and we saw a woman running across the marketplace. She was thin, covered with a shawl, carrying her huge pregnant belly in front of her. She ran after those who were walking away, her hand raised in a gesture of farewell, and we heard her voice. She was shouting, *"Zei gezint, Tate! Tate, zei gezint!"**

And then all of us hidden in the darkness began to repeat, *"Zeit gezint,"* bidding farewell with those words to our loved ones who were walking to their deaths.

* Be well, Papa, be well.

A
DOG

Our dog was named Ching. We called him that because on the day he appeared in our home all the front pages of the newspapers carried the first reports of the Sino-Japanese incident.

After much discussion—Rex? Lux? Ami?—we settled on the Chinese name—and not only because of current events, but the dog had a squint that made him look Chinese, or so Agata said. This made no sense—Agata had never seen a Chinese person—but her suggestion stuck.

"Of course," we cried out, "he's a Chinaman, he's got slanted eyes and he squints!"

"Chinese people don't squint," our older, fourteen-year-old cousin snapped.

"But they can," my sister argued.

"He's the spitting image of a Chinaman," said Agata, ending the discussion.

Ching, whose mother was Santuzza, a purebred fox terrier owned by the music-loving veterinarian, took after his father, and in just a few weeks it was clear that he was turning out to be a charming mutt. The only sign of his fox terrier blood was the shape of his muzzle, as our neighbor the judge, a self-appointed canine expert, assured us. We often cited his opinion when we took Ching out on his leash for a walk and the children shouted after us, "Mutt on a string!"

"But he has a fox terrier's head," we would answer proudly.

"And what about his behind?" said the kids.

Ching knew how to beg, how to shake hands, and how to fetch. He obeyed all our commands, without enthusiasm or joy, but rather with a sad air of resignation, a kind of philosophical thoughtfulness, which Agata was the first to notice. One day, when she was carrying in a platter of steaming pirogi, she announced: "That Ching is a philosopher . . ."

"Of what school?" our well-read cousin joked.

"A sad one," Agata replied.

The dog was definitely sad. He didn't run around the garden. He disdained toy bones, the special little ball he'd gotten as a gift, and even the chickens that scratched all day in the yard. He could usually be found on the couch, on the soft, woolly hand-woven throw. He would be watching a fly strolling on the windowpane, and in answer to our solicitous "Ching-ching, why are you so sad?" we would hear his soft, tender, clarinet-like voice.

When he was two years old he moved into the servants' quarters permanently. He slept with our housekeeper, which earned him a new nickname, "Agata's lover." Agata really did love him. Elderly, a spinster past her prime, she lavished all her affection on the squint-eyed dog, and fussed over him as if he were a baby—so much so, that she would hold the dog in her arms while making jam, with no regard for hygiene.

"He won't climb into the pot," she'd say, ignoring all our complaints, angry at our coldheartedness, which seemed to her a hundred times worse than failing to observe the rules of cleanliness.

During the war our interest in Ching cooled off dramatically, so that we hardly paid him any attention. But in the evening, when we were getting ready for bed, frightened of the coming night, and with our underwear and clothing laid out so we could get into it as quickly as possible, then Agata would appear in our room holding Ching in her arms like a child and say, "Ching, kiss them good night." And Ching would bark ever so softly and just barely wag his tail, and then he would lick our faces. It was an extremely irritating ceremony. What night could be good? Who had any patience for a dog? But since our cousin, who would have known how to stop Agata, was no longer around, having been killed during the first action, we endured it until Agata and Ching left for the country and we moved into the ghetto.

Before that, however, Ching gave us proof of his heartfelt loyalty. It was a test that many more people than animals failed in those days. On the day before both our moves there was another action in our town, longer than all the previous ones, and one that showed us how incredibly far cruelty and bestiality could go.

We hid, the seven of us, in a former pigsty, which—in addition to its other dubious virtues as a shelter—also lacked a door. In the past it must have had a door, perhaps even a strong one, as the arched entrance studded with hooks and nails suggested. A shelter without a door is sheer madness. But this was one of the things that helped save us. Had they seen a closed door, the Germans searching the yard and outbuildings would certainly have kicked it in, thus assuring a sentence of death in Belzec for the seven people seated on the hay that was still there from the time of the pigs. But since what they saw was a yawning black hole left by a broken door, a hole that was barely concealed by a pile of dry leafless branches, they passed it by with a clear conscience, not suspecting that people were hiding inside. The moment when the silhouette of an SS-man appeared in the pointed arch of the pigsty and his hand carelessly brushed the apple tree, dried by the summer heat—that moment gave us a taste of suspension in that limbo between life and death.

That Agata should have stubbornly answered their shouted demands with "I don't know, I don't know" was absolutely predictable—so predictable that we hardly appreciated it, as often happens with those who love us faithfully. But what about poor, sad, forgotten Ching?

They took him out of Agata's arms, warning her not to say one word to him, fed him kielbasa, which, starved as he was, he gladly gobbled up, and then asked him in a gentle voice to find his "master."

"Where's your master? . . . mistress? . . . master? . . . mistress? . . ."

Ching looked at them calmly (afterwards Agata swore that he shook his head no) and didn't even tremble. He just looked at them and sat there. But they kept urging him in broken Polish: "Find your master . . . find your mistress . . ." Then, for the first time in his life, energy welled up in him, and not only did he begin barking at the top of his lungs, he even nipped at the German's calf.

Crouched in the pigsty, we could clearly hear the negotiations between the SS-men and the dog, from which the latter emerged triumphant. It is true that he got kicked for this, but he bore this blow in silence, although afterwards he trembled for the rest of the day, just like a person who, after some extraordinary effort, cannot calm down for the longest time.

Fate brought Ching a tragic end. He died an inhuman death. It happened a year later, several days after our escape from the ghetto, and it had all the earmarks of a cruel and ordinary SS death. It happened at lunchtime on a summer day in Agata's brother-in-law's front yard.

After leaving our house, Agata had moved in with her relatives in the country. And it was there that the Germans found her, sitting in front of their hut. They had been searching for us frantically for three days and were furious that they could find no one to reward for turning in the family that had fled the ghetto, and that their searches in the homes of that family's Polish friends and acquaintances had yielded nothing.

Their conversation with Agata was the last straw. Their rage, fueled by powerlessness—a feeling intolerable to the *Herrenvolk*—had to find an outlet. In an instant they expanded the scope of the Nuremberg Laws, to apply not only to Jewish great-grandmothers but also to Jewish-owned dogs.

"You're going to hang in their place!" they shouted, and when she told us the story, Agata shouted, too, and added that the faces of the murderers were as red as the peonies in her brother-in-law's garden.

She had to fetch a rope. There wasn't any strong rope around, but a thin string sufficed, because the dog was skinny. When they whistled for him, he came readily, his body trembling, as usual. They hanged him from a branch of a cherry tree, and rode off on a motorcycle, lighter by one more death.

JEAN-CHRISTOPHE

We were working on the Ostbahn. It was a good work assignment because our *Aufseherin* was a girl we knew; we had gone to school with her. She was pretty then, round-faced, with curly dark hair. She used to sleep with the clerks in the district office, and now she slept with the Germans, but she was a good girl—she only slept with them, that's all. It was a good assignment: planting embankments wasn't hard work, and we were in the woods, in a beautiful forest some five or maybe eight kilometers outside of town, amid the silence of the trees. Also, this *Aufseherin* didn't much care what we did or how we worked. She just sat under a tree, bored. She would have loved to talk to us, but she was probably afraid of losing her job. She wasn't pretty anymore; she had grown heavy and her complexion was blotchy.

Sometimes, during our dinner break, she would sit near us and say, "This is a lovely forest, isn't it?"

"It *is* lovely," we would reply.

It was obvious that she was sensitive.

On the day of the action in town she was tactful enough not to ask why we weren't working, why our shovels and hoes lay under the tree. She sat at the edge of the clearing with her back to us. We were lying on the grass, not saying a word, waiting for the thundering of the train, because then we would know it was all over—though not, of course, who was on the train, who had been taken and who had been spared.

We lay on the grass, not saying a word, as if our voices could have drowned out the thundering of the train, which would pass near the edge of the forest, not far from where we were working. Only one girl was crying. She wasn't the youngest, and, in fact, she was the only one of us who had no one left in the town, who was all alone. She cried quietly, moaning every once in a while. No one tried to comfort her. Another girl was braiding wreaths—large clumps of bluebells grew everywhere—but every time she finished one she would rip it apart and begin all over again. She pulled up every bluebell in the clearing. Another girl was gnawing on some bread; she chewed it slowly, thoughtfully, and when she had eaten her ration she grabbed someone else's bread and kept chewing. The oldest girl kept putting her ear to the ground.

It was silent in the forest. There were no birds, but the smell of the trees and flowers was magnificent. We couldn't hear anything. There was nothing to hear. The silence was horrifying because we knew that there was shooting going on and people screaming and crying, that it was a slaughterhouse out there. But here there were bluebells, hazelwood, daisies, and other flowers, very pretty, very colorful. That was what was so horrifying—just as horrifying as waiting for the thundering of the train, as horrifying as wondering whom they had taken.

One of us, a thin, dark-haired girl, had moved slightly away from the group and lay in the shade of the hazel trees. She alone wasn't straining to hear anything; she just lay on her stomach, reading a book. We could hear the soft, steady rustle of pages being turned. Not once did she lift her head and look at us. The book was thick; it was falling apart. When a strong wind blew up in the afternoon—the train still had not thundered past—several pages were suddenly whipped into the air. And as they fluttered over us like doves, she ran around, crying, "Catch them!" Then she gathered up the pages, put the book back together, lay down on her stomach, propped herself up on her elbows, and began to read again.

The girl who had been crying was now sobbing louder; all of us were aware that every passing minute brought the train's thunder nearer, that any moment now we would hear death riding down the tracks. One girl cried "Mama!" and then other voices cried "Mama!" because there was an echo in the woods.

Our *Aufseherin* finished hemming a kerchief, tossed her empty cigarette box into the bushes, stood up, and began pacing. Once she stopped beside the thin, dark-haired girl, obviously wanting to ask her something; instead, she walked away, humming softly and repeatedly checking her watch.

But the next time she passed near the girl, she couldn't help herself. "What are you reading?" she asked.

With great reluctance, the girl tore herself away from her book and looked up.

"*Jean-Christophe.*"

"*Jean-Christophe?*" The *Aufseherin* was surprised. "The title's just *Jean-Christophe?*"

"*Jean-Christophe,*" the girl replied.

"Is it good?"

She nodded.

"Is it about love?"

The girl thought for a moment. She was very thin, she wore a man's jacket instead of a blouse, and she looked very ugly. She answered seriously, "Love? That too."

"About love!" The *Aufseherin* burst out laughing. Maybe she laughed because she liked love. "Will you lend it to me when you're done?"

"Why not?" she answered. "I'll give it to you to keep."

"No, not to keep; lend it to me and I'll return it." She thought for a moment. "It must be good—you've been reading it all day; and especially on a day like this when they're taking your people away."

"I have to hurry," said the girl. "I want to make sure I finish it in time. There's one more section, and I'm afraid I won't be able to finish it." She looked carefully at the book to see how many pages she had left. "I'm afraid I won't have time to finish it," she repeated, to herself now, but the *Aufseherin* heard her.

"It must be *very* good. What's it called? I forget . . ."

"*Jean-Christophe.*"

"*Jean-Christophe,*" she repeated several times, and explained, "If you're not around to lend it to me, I'll look for it in the library."

Then she felt sorry and added, "But I'm sure you'll finish it. It's not *that* long."

The girl who had been crying began sobbing still louder. It wasn't weeping anymore, it was lamentation. The oldest one of us knelt down and placed her ear to the earth. But the earth was still silent.

THE
KEY
GAME

They had just finished supper and the woman had cleared the table, carried the plates to the kitchen, and placed them in the sink. The kitchen was mottled with patches of dampness and had a dull, yellowish light, even gloomier than in the main room. They had been living here for two weeks. It was their third apartment since the start of the war; they had abandoned the other two in a hurry. The woman came back into the room and sat down again at the table. The three of them sat there: the woman, her husband, and their chubby, blue-eyed, three-year-old child. Lately they had been talking a lot about the boy's blue eyes and chubby cheeks.

The boy sat erect, his back straight, his eyes fixed on his father, but it was obvious that he was so sleepy he could barely sit up.

The man was smoking a cigarette. His eyes were bloodshot and he kept blinking in a funny way. This blinking had begun soon after they fled the second apartment.

It was late, past ten o'clock. The day had long since ended, and they could have gone to sleep, but first they had to play the game that they had been playing every day for two weeks and still had not got right. Even though the man tried his best and his movements were agile and quick, the fault was his and not the child's. The boy was marvelous. Seeing his father put out his cigarette, he shuddered and opened his blue eyes even wider. The woman, who didn't actually take part in the game, stroked the boy's hair.

"We'll play the key game just one more time, only today. Isn't that right?" she asked her husband.

He didn't answer because he was not sure if this really would be the last rehearsal. They were still two or three minutes off. He stood up and walked towards the bathroom door. Then the woman called out softly, "Ding-dong." She was imitating the doorbell and she did it beautifully. Her "ding-dong" was quite a soft, lovely bell.

At the sound of chimes ringing so musically from his mother's lips, the boy jumped up from his chair and ran to the front door, which was separated from the main room by a narrow strip of corridor.

"Who's there?" he asked.

The woman, who alone had remained in her chair, clenched her eyes shut as if she were feeling a sudden, sharp pain.

"I'll open up in a minute, I'm just looking for the keys," the child called out. Then he ran back to the main room, making a lot of noise with his feet. He ran in circles around the table, pulled out one of the sideboard drawers, and slammed it shut.

"Just a minute, I can't find them, I don't know where Mama put them," he yelled, then dragged the chair across the room, climbed onto it, and reached up to the top shelf of the étagère.

"I found them!" he shouted triumphantly. Then he got

down from the chair, pushed it back to the table, and without looking at his mother, calmly walked to the door. A cold, musty draft blew in from the stairwell.

"Shut the door, darling," the woman said softly. "You were perfect. You really were."

The child didn't hear what she said. He stood in the middle of the room, staring at the closed bathroom door.

"Shut the door," the woman repeated in a tired, flat voice. Every evening she repeated the same words, and every evening he stared at the closed bathroom door.

At last it creaked. The man was pale and his clothes were streaked with lime and dust. He stood on the threshold and blinked in that funny way.

"Well? How did it go?" asked the woman.

"I still need more time. He has to look for them longer. I slip in sideways all right, but then . . . it's so tight in there that when I turn . . . And he's got to make more noise—he should stamp his feet louder."

The child didn't take his eyes off him.

"Say something to him," the woman whispered.

"You did a good job, little one, a good job," he said mechanically.

"That's right," the woman said, "you're really doing a wonderful job, darling—and you're not little at all. You act just like a grown-up, don't you? And you do know that if someone should really ring the doorbell someday when Mama is at work, everything will depend on you? Isn't that right? And what will you say when they ask you about your parents?"

"Mama's at work."

"And Papa?"

He was silent.

"And Papa?" the man screamed in terror.

The child turned pale.

"And Papa?" the man repeated more calmly.

"He's dead," the child answered and threw himself at his father, who was standing right beside him, blinking his eyes in that funny way, but who was already long dead to the people who would really ring the bell.

A
SPRING
MORNING

During the night there was a pouring rain, and in the morning when the first trucks drove across the bridge, the foaming Gniezna River was the dirty-yellow color of beer. At least that's how it was described by a man who was crossing this bridge—a first-class reinforced concrete bridge —with his wife and child for the last time in his life. The former secretary of the former town council heard these words with his own ears: he was standing right near the bridge and watching the Sunday procession attentively, full of concern and curiosity. As the possessor of an Aryan great-grandmother he could stand there calmly and watch them in peace. Thanks to him and to people like him, there have survived to this day shreds of sentences, echoes of final laments, shadows of the sighs of the participants in the *marches funèbres*, so common in those times.

"Listen to this," said the former secretary of the former town council, sitting with his friends in the restaurant at the railroad station—it was all over by then. "Listen to this: Here's a man facing death, and all he can think about is beer. I was speechless. And besides, how could he say that?

I made a point of looking at it, the water was like water, just a little dirtier."

"Maybe the guy was just thirsty, you know?" the owner of the bar suggested, while he filled four large mugs until the foam ran over. The clock above the bar rattled and struck twelve. It was already quiet and empty in town. The rain had stopped and the sun had broken through the white puffs of clouds. The sizzle of frying meat could be heard from the kitchen. On Sunday, dinner should be as early as possible. It was clear that the SS shared that opinion. At twelve o'clock the ground in the meadow near the forest was trampled and dug up like a fresh wound. But all around it was quiet. Not even a bird called out.

When the first trucks rode across the bridge over the surging Gniezna, it was five in the morning and it was still completely dark, yet Aron could easily make out a dozen or so canvas-covered trucks. That night he must have slept soundly, deaf to everything, since he hadn't heard the rumbling of the trucks as they descended from the hills into the little town in the valley. As a rule, the rumbling of a single truck was enough to alert him in his sleep; today, the warning signals had failed him. Later, when he was already on his way, he remembered that he had been dreaming about a persistent fly, a buzzing fly, and he realized that that buzzing was the sound of the trucks riding along the high road above his house—the last house when one left the town, the first when one entered it.

They were close now, and with horrifying detachment

he realized that his threshold would be the first they crossed. "In a few minutes," he thought, and slowly walked over to the bed to wake his wife and child.

The woman was no longer asleep—he met her gaze immediately, and was surprised at how large her eyes were. But the child was lying there peacefully, deep in sleep. He sat down on the edge of the bed, which sagged under his weight. He was still robust, though no longer so healthy looking as he used to be. Now he was pale and gray, and in that pallor and grayness was the mark of hunger and poverty. And terror, too, no doubt.

He sat on the dirty bedding, which hadn't been washed for a long time, and the child lay there quietly, round and large and rosy as an apple from sleep. Outside, in the street, the motors had fallen silent; it was as quiet as if poppy seeds had been sprinkled over everything.

"Mela," he whispered, "is this a dream?"

"You're not dreaming, Aron. Don't just sit there. Put something on, we'll go down to the storeroom. There's a stack of split wood there, we can hide behind it."

"The storeroom. What a joke. If I thought we could hide in the storeroom we'd have been there long ago. In the storeroom or in here, it'll make no difference."

He wanted to stand up and walk over to the window, but he was so heavy he couldn't. The darkness was already lifting. He wondered, are they waiting until it gets light? Why is it so quiet? Why doesn't it begin?

"Aron," the woman said.

Again her large eyes surprised him, and lying there on the bed in her clothing—she hadn't undressed for the night —she seemed younger, slimmer, different. Almost the way she was when he first met her, so many years ago. He stretched out his hand and timidly, gently, stroked hers. She wasn't surprised, although as a rule he was stingy with caresses, but neither did she smile. She took his hand and squeezed it firmly. He tried to look at her, but he turned away, for something strange was happening inside him. He was breathing more and more rapidly, and he knew that in a moment these rapid breaths would turn into sobs.

"If we had known," the woman said softly, "we wouldn't have had her. But how could we have known? Smarter people didn't know. She'll forgive us, Aron, won't she?"

He didn't answer. He was afraid of this rapid breathing; he wanted only to shut his eyes, put his fingers in his ears, and wait.

"Won't she, Aron?" she repeated.

Then it occurred to him that there wasn't much time left and that he had to answer quickly, that he had to answer everything and say everything that he wanted to say.

"We couldn't know," he said. "No, we wouldn't have had her, that's clear. I remember, you came to me and said, 'I'm going to have a child, maybe I should go to a doctor.' But I wanted a child, I wanted one. And I said, 'Don't be afraid, we'll manage it somehow. I won't be any worse than a young father.' I wanted her."

"If only we had a hiding place," she whispered, "if we had a hiding place everything would be different. Maybe we should hide in the wardrobe, or under the bed. No . . . it's better to just sit here."

"A shelter is often just a shelter, and not salvation. Do you remember how they took the Goldmans? All of them, the whole family. And they had a good bunker."

"They took the Goldmans, but other people managed to hide. If only we had a cellar here . . ."

"Mela," he said suddenly, "I have always loved you very much, and if you only knew—"

But he didn't finish, because the child woke up. The little girl sat there in bed, warm and sticky from her child's sleep, and rosy all over. Serious, unsmiling, she studied her parents' faces.

"Are those trucks coming for us, Papa?" she asked, and he could no longer hold back his tears. The child knew! Five years old! The age for teddy bears and blocks. Why did we have her? She'll never go to school, she'll never love. Another minute or two . . .

"Hush, darling," the woman answered, "lie still, as still as can be, like a mouse."

"So they won't hear?"

"So they won't hear."

"If they hear us, they'll kill us," said the child, and wrapped the quilt around herself so that only the tip of her nose stuck out.

How bright her eyes are, my God! Five years old! They should be shining at the thought of games, of fun. Five! She knows, and she's waiting just like us.

"Mela," he whispered, so the child wouldn't hear, "let's hide her. She's little, she'll fit in the coalbox. She's little, but she'll understand. We'll cover her with wood chips."

"No, don't torture yourself, Aron. It wouldn't help. And what would become of her then? Who would she go to? Who would take her? It will all end the same way, if not now, then the next time. It'll be easier for her with us. Do you hear them?"

He heard them clearly and he knew: time was up. He wasn't afraid. His fear left him, his hands stopped trembling. He stood there, large and solid—breathing as if he were carrying an enormous weight.

It was turning gray outside the window. Night was slipping away, though what was this new day but night, the blackest of black nights, cruel, and filled with torment.

They were walking in the direction of the railroad station, through the town, which had been washed clean by the night's pouring rain and was as quiet and peaceful as it always was on a Sunday morning.

They walked without speaking, already stripped of everything human. Even despair was mute; it lay like a death mask, frozen and silent, on the face of the crowd.

The man and his wife and child walked along the edge of the road by the sidewalk; he was carrying the little girl in his arms. The child was quiet; she looked around solemnly, with both arms wrapped around her father's neck. The man and his wife no longer spoke. They had said their last words in the house, when the door crashed open, kicked in by the boot of an SS-man. He had said then to the child, "Don't be afraid, I'll carry you in my arms." And to his wife he said, "Don't cry. Let's be calm. Let's be strong and endure this with dignity." Then they left the house for their last journey.

For three hours they stood in the square surrounded by a heavy escort. They didn't say one word. It was almost as if they had lost the power of speech. They were mute, they were deaf and blind. Once, a terrible feeling of regret tore through him when he remembered the dream, that buzzing fly, and he understood that he had overslept his life. But this, too, passed quickly; it was no longer important, it couldn't change anything. At ten o'clock they set out. His legs were tired, his hands were numb, but he didn't put the child down, not even for a minute. He knew it was only

an hour or so till they reached the fields near the station—
the flat green pastures, which had recently become the
mass grave of the murdered. He also recalled that years ago
he used to meet Mela there, before they were husband and
wife. In the evenings there was usually a strong wind, and
it smelled of thyme.

The child in his arms felt heavier and heavier, but not
because of her weight. He turned his head slightly and
brushed the little girl's cheek with his lips. A soft, warm
cheek. In an hour, or two . . .

Suddenly his heart began to pound, and his temples were
drenched with sweat.

He bent towards the child again, seeking the strength
that flowed from her silky, warm, young body. He still
didn't know what he would do, but he did know that he
had to find some chink through which he could push his
child back into the world of the living. Suddenly he was
thinking very fast. He was surprised to see that the trees
had turned green overnight and that the river had risen;
it was flowing noisily, turbulently, eddying and churning;
on that quiet spring morning, it was the only sign of
nature's revolt. "The water is the color of beer," he said
aloud, to no one in particular. He was gathering up the
colors and smells of the world that he was losing forever.
Hearing his voice, the child squirmed and looked him in
the eye.

"Don't be afraid," he whispered, "do what Papa tells you.
Over there, near the church, there are a lot of people, they
are going to pray. They are standing on the sidewalk and
in the yard in front of the church. When we get there, I'm
going to put you down on the ground. You're little, no one
will notice you. Then you'll ask somebody to take you to
Marcysia, the milkmaid, outside of town. She'll take you in.

Or maybe one of those people will take you home. Do you understand what Papa said?"

The little girl looked stunned; still, he knew she had understood.

"You'll wait for us. We'll come back after the war. From the camp," he added. "That's how it has to be, darling. It has to be this way," he whispered quickly, distractedly. "That's what you'll do, you have to obey Papa."

Everything swam before his eyes; the image of the world grew blurry. He saw only the crowd in the churchyard. The sidewalk beside him was full of people, he was brushing against them with his sleeve. It was only a few steps to the churchyard gate; the crush of people was greatest there, and salvation most likely.

"Go straight to the church," he whispered and put the child down on the ground. He didn't look back, he didn't see where she ran, he walked on stiffly, at attention, his gaze fixed on the pale spring sky in which the white threads of a cloud floated like a spider web. He walked on, whispering a kind of prayer, beseeching God and men. He was still whispering when the air was rent by a furious shriek:

"*Ein jüdisches Kind!*"

He was still whispering when the sound of a shot cracked like a stone hitting water. He felt his wife's fingers, trembling and sticky from sweat; she was seeking his hand like a blind woman. He heard her faint, whimpering moan. Then he fell silent and slowly turned around.

At the edge of the sidewalk lay a small, bloody rag. The smoke from the shot hung in the air—wispy, already blowing away. He walked over slowly, and those few steps seemed endless. He bent down, picked up the child, stroked the tangle of blond hair.

"*Deine?*"

He answered loud and clear, "*Ja, meine.*" And then softly, to her, "Forgive me."

He stood there with the child in his arms and waited for a second shot. But all he heard was a shout and he understood that they would not kill him here, that he had to keep on walking, carrying his dead child.

"Don't be afraid, I'll carry you," he whispered. The procession moved on like a gloomy, gray river flowing out to sea.

A

CONVERSATION

When he entered her room and slowly, carefully closed the door, and then began pacing the two steps between the window and the table, she realized that something had happened, and she guessed that it had to do with Emilia.

She was sitting beside the stove because it was already winter, which meant that almost six months had gone by since Emilia had taken them in. She rested her feet on a bundle of firewood that Michal had split, and softly clicked her knitting needles. She was making a stocking out of black sheep's wool. Emilia had taught her how to do that; she hadn't known how to knit before. She was grateful to her because she could do something useful—fill this unproductive time to which she had been condemned, isolated from the world and from people, imprisoned in this tiny room. At first, she had been grateful to Emilia for everything, and she was grateful to her now, too, but in a different way, in an abstract, cool, cerebral way.

Everything made her nervous: her husband's footsteps; his high, mud-caked boots; his jacket, which belonged to Emilia's husband, who had been missing since the start of the war; his sunburned face, which was also not his own, because in the past he had always been so pale—that pale, Slavic face, so unusual in his swarthy, black-haired family.

Because he was making her nervous, and not to make it easier for him, she asked him first, without raising her head, which was bent over the needles:

"Is it about Emilia?"

"What makes you think that?"

The rough way he asked and the fact that he was standing perfectly still convinced her that she was right.

"Because I know. I have a lot of time, I think about things. I knew from the beginning that this would happen. Once I was standing near the window—don't be afraid, no one saw me—and I watched her. I saw how she looked at you, how she moved, her smile, it was completely obvious."

"Not to me. I had no idea until . . ."

"Why are you so upset? Calm down. You say you didn't know about it until . . ."

"Put down the needles," he said, furious. "I can't stand that clicking. And look at me, I can't talk like this."

"The clicking is what keeps me calm. It's a wonderful thing, this soft, monotonous clicking. I can talk while I'm doing it. You'd be surprised what I can do. So you had no idea . . ."

"Anna, why are you acting like this?"

"So you had no idea until . . ."

"Until she told me herself."

"How touching! And what did she tell you?"

"She just told me."

"That she can't take it anymore, that you are always together, and that since 1939, when her husband didn't return from the war, she has lived alone—poor thing. Is that right?"

"How did you know?"

"I told you, I just know. When did it happen?"

"A month ago."

"A month ago. And for a whole month you went on being together from dawn till night, together in the fields, together gathering wood in the forest, together going to town on errands . . . You know what? You really do look terrific, and she's very sharp, she spotted it right away that first evening. 'You can pretend to be my cousin, you're a born estate manager.' I never saw you as an estate manager, but that's probably because I never saw an estate manager in my whole life, I only read about them. She also sized me up right away. 'With your face, not one step outside this door . . .' "

"You're being unfair, Anna, ungrateful. . . ."

"I know. And have you and she . . . ? You can tell me."

"No."

He stood there in his mud-caked boots and Emilia's husband's jacket, leaning against the wall, sunburned and so tall that his head almost reached the ceiling. He smells of fresh air, she thought. And also, he has changed, he's not the same man.

"Stop it!" he shouted. "Put that stocking down! We're leaving, we have to leave. Now, today, at once!"

She didn't want the sound of the needles to stop, but they fell out of her hands. A soft, almost imperceptible shiver ran through her. She recognized it.

"Leave? Why?" she asked in a frightened voice, and immediately began to shake. Earlier, before Emilia took them in, she used to shake like that constantly.

"Why, Michal?"

He didn't answer.

"Michal, why? Is she driving us out?"

"We have to leave, Anna."

"But Michal, for God's sake, where to? We have nowhere to go, we have no one. With my face, without money . . . I won't survive, you know it. Talk to her, ask her . . ."

Suddenly she raised her head and looked into his eyes. For a moment she seemed about to scream. She looked panic-stricken, horrified; then just as suddenly she lowered her eyes and straightened up. She was no longer trembling. She sat stiffly, and in her black dress, with her smoothly combed black hair, she looked like a nun. She picked up the stocking from the floor and set the needles in motion: her white hands began to dance rapidly and rhythmically to the beat of the metal sticks. She pressed her lips into a horizontal, dark-blue line.

"All right," she said after a moment.

Because her head was bowed, she didn't, couldn't see the flush that passed across the man's face and left it a shade paler. But she heard his loud breathing.

"All right. You can tell her that everything's all right."

"Anna . . ."

"Please go now."

At the sound of the door closing she trembled slightly, but she did not put down her work or raise her eyes. She sat stiff and straight, the needles clicked softly. After a moment, her lips moved silently. She was counting her stitches.

THE

BLACK

BEAST

I was standing in the doorway, my hand still on the latch, when I saw him watching me. At first I saw nothing else; he drew all my attention. He looked at me intently, hostilely. I took this hostility as a bad sign. It's bad, I thought, not taking my eyes off him, the old man won't take me in. That's what I thought; but out loud I praised the name of God. I knew that the old man was there in the hut, sitting at the table, the smoke from his pipe was hurting my eyes. I knew this without seeing him.

A deep voice responded with "May He be praised forever." Only then did I tear my gaze from the huge form sitting next to the stove and focus on the owner of the place. He was a small, bony man, with bushy eyebrows. Matilda had described him perfectly, even the ugly hairy mole on his cheek, and the gray, twisted moustache that curled downwards. That was him, Matilda's uncle. So I announced that I had come from his niece in Dobrowka and that I was asking for a roof over my head for a week or two. There was a silence. The only sound was the panting of that black beast that I was afraid to look at. A branch was tapping at the window, and outside the night was dark and cold.

I took the pack off my shoulders; my legs felt so tired I sat down uninvited on the bench beside the door. The dog slurped loudly; it sounded as if he were giving permission and I sighed with relief.

"What a rogue that Tilda is! I didn't know she was hiding Jews." The old man laughed. The word he used to describe his niece was as inappropriate as his laughter. Anyone who had ever seen Matilda—a retired school-teacher, a tall, dignified woman—would have bridled at that, as I did. A rogue! Was he making fun of her?

"You been staying with her a long time, Mister?"

"Six months."

"So why is she sending you to me now?"

"She's afraid of a search, she's asking for a week or two."

"She didn't give you a letter?"

"She didn't want to, because if they had found it on me . . ."

"Well, that's absolutely right. Did you come on foot?"

"Yes."

"It's a long way. No one saw you?"

"I made it. But I was very frightened."

"Sure. I'd have been frightened, too, in your shoes. I'm pretty fearful, as a rule."

"Matilda said you wouldn't refuse."

"I wouldn't refuse? And why's that? Matilda always knows better than everyone else. Won't refuse? Of course I'll refuse."

He was arguing with her, not with me; it didn't sound too alarming. But a moment later he added seriously, "I can't."

He said it gently, almost regretfully. I understood that he was afraid and I got up from the bench. The dog, that black beast lying near the stove, jumped up on its sturdy legs. I don't know what breed it was, probably a mutt; heavy-boned, stocky, it resembled a wolf. It moved from the corner to the center of the hut, sniffed my legs, and growled softly. "He'd give me away," I thought, "that black beast would betray me." I took my pack from the floor and threw it over my shoulder. I didn't have the faintest idea where I'd go.

"Just a minute, just a minute," the old man said. "I won't let you go without some supper." He thought for a moment, then latched the door and hung a blanket over the window. "You can spend the night here with me. But only tonight."

Later he led me up to the attic. He stood in the passage, lighting the way with a lantern, and I climbed up the narrow, rotting ladder. I was on the top rung, just about to squeeze through the hatchway from which came the cloying smell of hay, when I looked behind me. Down below stood the dog, his head thrown back; he was keeping an eye on me.

A moment later I was lying in the hay, exhausted, half conscious, worn out from walking all day, and from terror. Even now the thought of my journey made me tremble. I marveled at the miraculous way I had managed to safely walk the fifteen kilometers from Dobrowka to Matilda's uncle's hut.

I didn't think about tomorrow. From below came the sounds of the old man's footsteps as he moved restlessly about the room; then they subsided and I sank into silence and sleep.

Suddenly I shuddered and woke up. My sharp, practiced ear had caught the sound of soft, almost inaudible steps. I froze in horror, even though I knew it was the dog. He climbed the ladder carefully, slowly, I could hear him breathing quietly. I recalled his hostile look, his enormous, heavy body, and what I had once read: they grab you by the throat. I crouched in the corner, cold sweat pouring down my face, I covered my face with my hands. When at last I lowered my hands, they were completely wet. The dog stood on the top rung of the ladder with his front paws resting on the sill of the loft. Two green flames were glowing at me. Drained by my needless panic, I said quietly, "Get out of here, go!" He turned obediently and ran down.

Early in the morning—I guessed it was morning by the strip of light streaming in through a crack in the roof—Matilda's uncle put a pan of milk and some bread down in front of me without saying a word.

"Do I have to go?" I asked. He didn't answer.

He never spoke to me, and if it weren't for the food that he left near the loft door twice a day one might think he didn't know I existed. But the black beast—that's how I thought of him—looked in on me every night when the hut grew still. He would silently climb the ladder and stand on the top rung with his eyes glowing. He would stand there till I said go away. I got used to those visits and after a week, I even waited for them. But it never entered my mind to call the dog although now, after everything that's happened, I think he expected me to and was waiting for it. Clearly, the terror that he aroused in me that first night was still with me, and my distrust had merely been lulled. One night I waited in vain. He didn't come. I waited a long time, and later had trouble falling asleep.

"What happened to the dog?" I asked the hand that slipped me the pot of milk the next morning.

"Matilda has sent word that you can go back."

It didn't even occur to me that he hadn't answered my question. I was overcome with emotion—joy at the thought of returning to kindly Matilda and my safe hiding place, and fear of the journey back.

The road wasn't safe. It led right through a large village, Siniawka, and there was no way around it. I left the loft filled with good and bad feelings.

When I thanked Matilda's uncle for his hospitality, he mumbled something into his whiskers. Only after I had already set off, he shouted after me, "Hurry, so you can walk through Siniawka before the fog lifts."

The fresh air startled me. I grabbed the fence and breathed deeply. It was very early, still dawn, and there was a thick fog. I closed the gate carefully and set out. I was trying to walk jauntily, which wasn't easy. For weeks I had been confined to two square meters, and now the open space terrified me. I suddenly regretted that I hadn't taken a stick with me, a walking stick. I could have used it to set a rhythm, I could have leaned on it. I was so busy thinking of the stick I didn't have that I went a good twenty meters or so before I heard those familiar, soft steps. I turned around; he had run after me.

"Goodbye, dog," I said, and for the first time, touched his coat. It felt warm and pleasant. He stretched his back beneath my hand, yawned loudly, and then, seized with a sudden rush of energy, shook as if after a bath and looked up at me.

"Get out of here! Go home, I have to go on," I said, but he didn't budge and followed me with his eyes. It was obvious that he was telling me something that people who understand the language of dogs would have understood.

But I had had very little to do with dogs and it never crossed my mind that you could talk to them.

Annoyed, I quickened my pace, but the dog, who used to be so obedient when I chased him from the loft, didn't listen. He trotted along beside me, rubbing against my legs from time to time. We walked in step, arm in arm, if you can use that expression—and you can, you really can, I know that now for a fact. I didn't know his name, so I called him simply "Dog."

I still hadn't figured out what he was up to. As we neared the place where the path through the meadow joined the highway, I assumed that here we would say goodbye. I was grateful to him for keeping me company on the first part of the trip, which was safer than what would follow—but more difficult, because the first minutes of solitude are always the loneliest. Luckily, one can get used to anything —it's one of the peculiar blessings fate bestowed on us in a moment of kindness.

The walk across the immense meadow was the beginning of my utter aloneness in the midst of that hostile world. Now, approaching the highway where I expected to say farewell, I realized that the grief that overcame me when I set out on my journey, the grief at not having a stick to lean on, was the desolate cry of a soul who has been abandoned by everyone.

This is what I was brooding about as I stood beside the ditch that divided the reddish autumn grass from the bumpy roadway. The fog was lifting, the sky was growing brighter, turning pink.

"Now go home, your master is waiting, go home, go home," I told the dog, who was running back and forth sniffing the ground along the deep ditch filled with rain-water.

"Enough, that's enough, go home," I called to him softly and pointed to the path that we had just left.

He paid no attention. He rooted in the ground, pawed at the grass, and suddenly bounded across the ditch. Now he was standing on the road, swinging his tail like a pendulum. He began to bark, and—a miracle!—I understood. "Jump," he was saying, "jump quickly!"

I stood as if fixed to the ground. But since he had jumped the ditch, since he was telling me to jump . . . I got a running start and flew across the filthy water and landed next to him on the road. I bent over and reached to stroke him. But he didn't want affection, he was in a hurry, he was already running straight ahead with his tail in the air. I had a hard time catching up with him.

The sun was shining, the first wagons appeared on the road. Their rumbling disturbed the early morning silence but not the peace I felt within me now because of the soft footsteps beside me. Only when the sun had risen higher and I looked down and saw the houses of Siniawka scattered about the valley did my serenity waver. But since we had already gone a good part of the distance, I left the road, and with him following me obediently, headed towards a grove to rest. I sat down, leaned against a tree, and the dog crouched down a few meters away from me. He was curious about his surroundings; he pricked up his ears, turned his head to the right, then to the left, and rhythmically thumped the ground with his strong tail. I was struck by his alert expression, which had so frightened me that first night and which I had foolishly thought hostile. Now, knowing him better, I read it differently—as heightened awareness, preparedness, a way of defending himself against surprises. I should have been turning *my* head from side to side, pricking up *my* ears on the alert. Instead, I sat there dully, worn out by the walk, wheezing slightly, my eyelids drooping sleepily.

"Listen," I said. He slowly turned his head towards me, baring his sharp, white fangs. "Listen, I'm going to take a little nap." I don't know if I said those words out loud or only thought them. Maybe I mumbled them, for I felt myself sinking into a warm whirlpool of sleep, falling into a blissful but not quite boundless abyss; I had slipped from a sitting position and was painfully aware of every place my body touched the ground.

The sleep that overwhelmed me so suddenly couldn't have been very deep since I could hear my own snoring— too loud for someone in my situation, and unwise. While I was sleeping I could see with perfect clarity the birch grove and the dog crouching beside me, keeping guard. And I was thinking very fast for a person deep in sleep, I was thinking that I could rest for just an hour, that I could postpone the difficult encounter with Siniawka for just an hour, since the dog was guarding me so diligently. But no sooner had I thought this than the dog jumped up and, with its tail down, raced towards the road. He was running away. I called to him, but since I didn't know his name I just said "dog" or "black beast." He was already disappearing from sight, getting smaller and smaller, first a patch of black, then a black stripe leaping along the road. I wasn't terribly sad at his sneaking off, I didn't have time, nor did I have room for sadness in me, I was too full of clammy terror at being alone once more.

I must have started in my sleep and shouted, because at the moment of waking my mouth was filled with sound and my face was wet. The black beast was standing over me, whimpering softly. He lifted his paw and gently touched my arms, once and then again.

We passed through Siniawka without incident. I didn't move stealthily between the fences as I did when I came through there the first time. We walked down the high road through the center of the village, in full view of everyone. The kids shouted, "What a big dog!" or, "Jesus! How black he is!" That "black" might have meant me, too, it might have led to another, more dangerous word. It might have. But I had a dog, I wasn't alone, and people like me didn't have dogs. I walked with the dignified pace of a farmer who has set out with his dog to visit a neighboring village.

We reached Dobrowka at four. Now I had to wait until sundown so I could sneak into Matilda's house under cover of darkness. We waited in the rushes by the pond. The frogs were croaking. The dog, sensing that our journey was ending, lay down at my feet and napped. From time to time he would lift his head and look at me, and then, reassured, would go back to sleep.

Late in the evening we walked up to Matilda's house. I ran up the stairs to the high porch and knocked at the window, as we had agreed. The door opened slightly and Matilda's tall, stern figure appeared in the doorway.

"Thank God. I was so worried about you."

"Matilda, please, give him something to eat, he's sitting there in the yard, he's hungry, you must have something."

"Who? What's wrong?"

"The dog."

She looked at me as if I were out of my mind.

"What dog? Please shut the door immediately, come in, quickly."

"He's sitting down there, next to the stairs. Your uncle's dog. He kept me company the whole way. Thanks to him I . . ."

I grasped her hand, she didn't believe me, she thought I was delirious. We ran down the stairs to the yard, but the yard was empty.

ARYAN PAPERS

The girl arrived first and sat down in the back of the room near the bar. Loud conversation, the clinking of glasses, and shouts from the kitchen hurt her ears; but when she shut her eyes, it sounded almost like the ocean. Smoke hung in the air like a dense fog and curled towards the roaring exhaust fan. Most of the customers were men and most of them were drinking vodka. The girl ordered tea, but the waiter, who had no experience with drinks of that sort, brought beer. It was sweet and smelled like a musty barrel. She drank, and the white foam clung to her lips. She wiped them brusquely with the back of her hand; in her anxiety she had forgotten her handkerchief.

Perhaps he won't come, she thought, relieved, then instantly terrified, because if he didn't come that would be the end of everything. Then she began to worry that someone would recognize her and she wished she could hide behind the curtain hanging over the door to the toilet.

When he entered, her legs began to tremble and she had to press her heels against the floor to steady herself.

"Good, you're here already," said the man and took off his coat.

"A double vodka!" he shouted towards the bar, "and hurry!"

He was tall, well built, with a suntanned face; his cheeks were a bit jowly, but he was good-looking. He was in his forties. He was nicely dressed, with a tasteful, conservative tie. When he picked up the glass she noticed that his fingernails were dirty.

"Well?" he asked, and glanced at the girl, who looked like a child in her plain, dark-blue raincoat. Her black eyes, framed by thick brows and lashes, were beautiful.

She swallowed hard and said, "Fine."

"Good," he said, smiling. "You see? The wolf is sated and the sheep is whole. As if there was a reason for all that fuss! Everything could have been taken care of by now."

He sat half turned away from her and looked at her out of the corner of his eye.

"Would you like something to eat? This place is disgusting but you must understand that I couldn't take you anywhere else. In a crummy bar like this even the informers are soused."

"I'm not hungry."

"You're nervous." He laughed again.

Her legs were still trembling as if she had just walked miles; she couldn't make them stay still.

"Come on, let's eat. This calls for a celebration."

"No."

She was afraid that she would pass out; she felt weak, first hot, then cold. She wanted to get everything over with as quickly as possible.

"Do you have it ready, sir? I brought the money . . ."

"What's this 'sir' business? We've already clinked glasses and you still call me sir! You're really something! Yes, I have everything ready. Signed and sealed. No cheating— the seals, the birth certificate—*alles in Ordnung!* Waiter, the check!"

He took her arm and she thought that it would be nice to have someone who would take her by the arm. Anyone but him.

The street was empty and dark; only after they reached the square did the streetlamps light the darkness and the passersby become visible. She expected that they would take a tram to save time, but they passed the stop and went on by foot.

"How old are you, sixteen?"

"Yes."

"For a sixteen-year-old you're definitely too thin and too short. But I like thin girls. I don't like fat on women. I knew you were my type the day you came to work. And I knew right away what you were. Who made those papers for you? What a lousy job. With mine you could walk through fire. Even with eyes like yours. How much did your mother give him?"

"Who?"

"The guy who's blackmailing you."

"She gave him her ring."

"A large one?"

"I don't know."

"One karat? Two?"

"I don't know. It was pretty. Grandma's."

"Aha, Grandma's. Probably a big stone. Too bad. So you see, I noticed at once that you had a problem, but I didn't know that you would admit it right away. At any rate, it's good that you happened to find me. I like to help people. Everybody wants to live. But why the hell did you spill it so fast?"

"I didn't care anymore."

"That's just talk! You knew I liked you, didn't you?"

"Maybe. I don't know."

"And why did your mother let the papers out of her hands?"

"They said that they wanted to check something and they took them away."

"And they said that they'd give them back once she came up with some cash. Right?" He laughed. "Was it always the same guys who came?"

"Yes."

"Naturally. Once you pay the first time, they'll keep coming back. They must have been making a pile. How much time did they give you?"

"Till the day after tomorrow. But we don't have any more money—really. The money I've brought for you is all we have."

He steered her through a gate and up to the third floor. The stairs were filthy and stank of urine.

"That means you want to leave tomorrow." And he added, "Send me your address and I'll come to see you; I've taken a liking to you."

The room was clean and neatly furnished. She looked at the white iron bed on which lay a pair of men's pajamas with cherry-red stripes.

If I throw up, she thought, he'll chase me out of here and it will all be for nothing.

"Please give me the documents, sir, I'll get the money out right away," she said.

"Sir? When you go to bed with someone, he's not a sir! Put your money away, we have time."

It probably doesn't take long, she thought. I'm not afraid of anything. Mama will be happy when I bring the papers. I should have done it a week ago. We would already be in Warsaw. I was stupid. He's even nice, he was always nice to me at work, and he could have informed.

"Don't just stand there, little one."

He sat down on the bed and took off his shoes. When he took off his trousers and carefully folded them along the crease, she turned her head away.

"I'll turn off the light," she said.

She heard his laughter and she felt flushed.

An hour later there was a knock at the door.

"Who's there?" he shouted from the bed.

"It's me, I've got business for you, open up!"

"The hell with you, what a time for business! What's up?"

"I'm not going to talk through the door. Do you have someone in there?"

"Yes."

"It's important and it ought to be taken care of fast. They could steal it from under our noses, and it would be too bad to lose all that good money."

"Get dressed," said the man. "You heard, someone's here on business. A man doesn't have a moment's rest! Don't put on such a mournful face, there's nothing to be sorry about! You'll be a terrific woman someday! Here you are, the birth certificates, the *Kennkarten*."

He counted skillfully, without licking his fingers. She could barely stand, and once again she felt queasy. She put the documents in her bag, the man opened the door and patted her on the shoulder. The other man, who was sitting on the stairs, turned around and looked at them with curiosity.

"Who's the girl?" he asked, entering the room.

"Oh, just a whore."

"I thought she was a virgin," he said, surprised. "Pale, teary-eyed, shaky . . ."

"Since when can't virgins be whores?"

"You're quite a philosopher," the other man said, and they both burst out laughing.

INSPECTOR VON GALOSHINSKY

He leaned against the door that had just shut and listened to the dull, ragged beating of his heart. The cell was dark, airless, thick with stale breath. At first he couldn't see anything, he could only hear the heavy breathing. But as he got used to the dark, he could make out the wooden planks that lined the walls and the small space that separated him from the door. He felt a sharp pain in his ribs and a weakness in his legs. He knew he couldn't keep standing much longer; and it was getting harder to breathe, but still he didn't move. From the darkness came a voice asking why he didn't lie down; then another, inquiring as to his name and how he had come to be there. He couldn't speak. His heart pounded dully, skipping beats; when it did that he felt he was going to faint. He finally roused himself and groped for an empty space on the bunk. He pulled himself up with effort, lay down on his right side so as to minimize the pain, and ordered himself: be calm. This was the final task of his life. He wanted to perform it conscientiously, to give his remaining time some human, moral significance. His lips were dry and cracked, it was all he could do to whisper: be calm, control yourself. When he ordered himself to be calm and self-controlled, did he really mean: be brave and dignified? He shut his eyes in order to concentrate, to lock himself into his thoughts, to shake off the numbness that reduces a man to a trapped animal. There wasn't much time, and he wanted to say an unhurried goodbye to his life. His heart slowed down, he was breathing more easily. This he noted, even though he was perfectly aware that the functioning of his body no longer mattered. He knew that Jews caught using Aryan papers were now shot within forty-eight hours. He had a last night and last day before him.

He wondered how much time had passed since they came for him. It seemed like a fraction of a second; everything had run together. That distant day a month ago, the last time he was with Teresa, surfaced in his memory, vivid, as if it were yesterday. The stairwell was so dark he could hardly see Teresa standing in the doorway. She said, "I want you to be with me, I don't want to be separated. Come back and stay with me."

"I'll come back. I can't go on like this anymore, either," he had answered.

He had stopped again half a flight down and looked up; she was gone. Why did you walk away so fast, he thought, I wanted to see you one more time. That's what had gone through his mind, and he'd felt a sudden pain in his heart, because those words sounded ominous.

A moment later he'd laughed at them, and at his stupid heart. He strode down the street, armed with his Aryan birth certificate, his employment papers from a German firm, and the pince-nez that had replaced his eyeglasses since his first day as an Aryan. That had been his one concession to his new life. Otherwise he lived normally, without any special precautions. His very Jewish appearance demanded either that he hide underground or cultivate an insane self-confidence. For two years he had been living like a madman with unfailing good luck.

"Where did they catch you?"

He opened his eyes and searched for the man who asked. Now he could see their faces, so similar in their pallor and exhaustion. They lay crowded together, with burnt-out eyes, seared by the fever of the life they had lost.

"They came to get me at work," he answered. "I tried to run away, but I tripped over something in the street and fell. If not for that, they wouldn't have caught me."

At the same time he was thinking, So it's with them that I'll be sharing the last bit of my life, their screams will be the last voices, the voices that will end the world for me.

"Who squealed on you?"

He was surprised by the question. He hadn't thought of that until this moment, and even now, when he reviewed in his mind the looks he had gotten recently, he found no answer.

"I don't know. I lived on the other side for two years and no one ever tried to trip me up." Then he added, "I was supposed to move to another city next week."

They laughed. Laughter was the last thing he would have expected. But in a moment he understood; their laughter was a sign of contempt.

"So you weren't in the ghetto? You didn't gasp for breath in a bunker? You didn't hear them shooting at your family? They didn't pull down your trousers? You are fresh, but the thirty of us here are well on our way to rotting by now."

He searched the darkness in vain; he couldn't see who was speaking. He figured that the guy must be young; he had a clear, mocking voice. How amazing that someone like that—someone whose strength you could sense—could wind up here, couldn't manage to save himself. But he remembered immediately that in these matters youth and strength made no difference. Everything was governed by accident and blind luck, which had granted him two years of relative peace.

"When was the last time they took people away?" he asked.

They were silent; he had touched their common wound. After a moment someone answered: "Four days ago. They used to take people every other day, but now they're liquidating the ghetto. The *Ordnungsdienst* said that the jail will go last."

They had been waiting four days! Suddenly the pain returned; it slammed him onto his back.

"You'll get used to it," that same young voice said. "You've just got to not give a damn, then you'll go to the killing grounds as light as a feather. True, it's harder for you—but we . . . we have experience."

He lay there with his face pressed into his shoulder and told himself, I'll think about Teresa, I'll think about everything that was beautiful and good in my life. It's the only way to protect myself. I'll think that way until the end. "Teresa," he whispered, "I want to say goodbye to you, I want you to be with me at the very end."

But he didn't see her, he saw only darkness, and whirling, reddish-yellow circles. He couldn't recall features that he knew by heart. He said to himself, "She has blond hair, she is tall and slender, she has a scar on her cheek . . ." But she did not appear, and that was horrible. He tried to jog his memory by summoning up the day she had entered his life; he remembered every detail: the raspberry ice cream in the little blue dishes, her green dress and white shoes; he saw the face of the waiter who said, "I can tell you're in love," although they weren't at all in love yet. But he did not see Teresa. It was torment, but he preferred to torture himself rather than die without a glimpse of her.

He heard himself say, "You're better off without me. You're blond, you look Polish, I look so Semitic." That was on the day when the regulation about the armbands was announced. They were both sitting in the room, with the light off, and Teresa was crying.

"It will be better that way," he said. "You'll go away, you'll be alone, it won't even occur to anyone. I'll come once a month."

"By train? You?" she asked—and he could still hear her pleading with him, "I can't, I won't be able to . . ."

But he forced her to do it, she went away, and he came once a month, just as he had promised. This time he was supposed to stay. They wanted to fix up the apartment; he had worked out a plan for a hiding place in the bathroom, just in case. Now what would happen if Teresa, worried by his silence and absence, came to the office and asked about him? Or showed up at his apartment? He bit his lip to keep from groaning.

He pictured her little alarm clock on the shelf. It says 8:00 P.M. The train he always takes arrives then. Teresa stands by the window and looks out at the street from behind the curtains. There is a bakery opposite the window, and chestnut trees line the sidewalk. A month ago they had buds on them—they must be green now. Teresa stands and looks, her eyes bright with joy. Then they grow dark, and she raises her hand to her mouth, as she always does when something frightens her. He can see her! At last he can see her. "Teresa!" he whispers, "take care of yourself, you have to survive . . ."

He felt the touch of someone's hand and shuddered as if he'd been awakened from sleep.

"Have they interrogated you?"

"No."

"They interrogate everyone, so don't be frightened."

"Where? Here?"

"Every day at ten Inspector von Galoshinsky makes his rounds."

"A German?"

"Of course he's German. Haven't you heard of him? He's well known in the ghetto. An oddball, a sadist. That's why I wanted to warn you."

"Did he interrogate you, too?"

"Yes."

He wanted to ask for details, but he felt enormously tired and longed to return to silence and solitude. He tried to find Teresa awaiting his arrival, but he had lost her. And not only her; everything had sunk into darkness, had vanished like smoke, irretrievable and unreal. Everything from over there. What remained was the darkness of the stinking cell, the people with whom he had to die, and this Galoshinsky.

"Calm down," he whispered, "so what if there's an interrogation? As long as it's fast, as long as I don't have to wait."

He didn't wait long. Footsteps echoed in the corridor, the cell door shook as someone kicked it with his boot. He jumped up and peered out; he didn't want to miss the moment when the door would open.

A powerful, booming voice searched out new arrivals: "*Ist jemand zugekommen?*"

"*Jawohl*," came the regulation response.

"Galoshinsky"—the whisper ran through the cell. He pulled himself together, enough to stop trembling.

"New people step forward!"

He slid down from the bunk and straightened his aching body. I am calm, Teresa, he said silently, and suddenly he saw her clearly beside him. She was smiling, squinting slightly, the wind was blowing her hair, and she held a large colored ball in her hands. A snapshot from our last vacation, he thought.

"To the middle of the cell, facing me," thundered Galoshinsky's voice.

He faced the closed door. A weak yellow light clicked on above, illuminating only the center of the cell. The bunks were in semidarkness.

"Name!"

He answered. He was still waiting for the moment when the door would open. He looked hard and saw an eye peering through the judas hole in the cell door.

"What are you?"

"I am a draftsman."

"You are a Jewish swine!" The voice grew louder; it was deafening. "Again! What are you?"

He took a deep breath.

"I am a Jew."

"I'll show you what you are. Lie down!"

Before he knew it he was lying down. The cement floor chilled him; it was damp and it stank.

"Stand up! Lie down! Stand up! Lie down!"

What for? he asked himself, but he couldn't control his body, and he bounced up and down like a ball. A hammer was beating in his temples; he no longer knew if it was his heart or that horrible booming voice.

"Dance! Do you hear? Dance, or I'll shoot! *Ein jüdisches Tanzele! Eins, zwei, drei!* Clap your hands! Faster, faster!"

I am a toy, a wound-up top, I want to stop and cannot. He was drenched with sweat, burning up.

"Stop! Take your clothes off! Strip naked! *Schneller, schneller!*"

Those weren't his hands flinging off his jacket, tearing at his trousers and underwear; that wasn't him standing naked.

"When was the last time you slept with your Sarah? Answer!"

Teresa! He called to her to help him and suddenly he grew sober.

"Answer, or I'll kill you like a dog!"

He stood motionless and looked straight ahead. He still couldn't make a sound, but he felt calm. My God, he said to himself, how could I, and for what?

"Answer me," boomed the voice, "or I'll shoot."

"Shoot!" he screamed. He stopped standing at attention and relaxed.

It grew quiet. He heard the rapid breathing of the prisoners and a faint whisper behind him.

"Shoot!" he screamed again. Now he was giving the orders, he was demanding. He didn't take his eyes off the judas hole; when the shot came, he wanted to be conscious, dignified, a human being.

The silence continued. Not even a rustle could be heard from outside the door. Then a thin ripple of laughter reached him. It was coming from deep inside the cell, growing bolder and more distinct. He turned around abruptly. The prisoners' amused faces were glowing; they could barely contain their laughter.

Suddenly he understood. He threw himself at the bunks like a madman.

A young prisoner was lying on the lowest bunk, in a dark corner with the cut-off top of a black galosh still in his mouth. He realized: Inspector von Galoshinsky! He raised his arm to swing at him, but his arm felt heavy and he lowered it.

"Animal!" he spat out.

He ran to his bunk, threw himself onto it, and hid his face in his hands.

"Hey you, new guy! Listen, don't make it into a tragedy. Put your clothes back on. Where's your sense of humor? After you've sat here a while you'll laugh like the rest of us. You can't imagine the kinds of things people say! About themselves, about their women. And nobody's caught on . . . You're the first to spoil the game. Do you know who banged on the door and turned on the light? Who was looking through the judas hole? The *Ordnungsdienst*; they get a kick out of it, too."

"How could you," he screamed. "You . . . you . . ."

"How could we? Another day or two and we'll all be feeding the worms."

They took them out that same night, just before dawn. The stars were already growing pale, the smell of spring was in the air. But they could not see the sky, they could not feel the wind. A canvas cover hid the world. When the truck started rolling more smoothly, they realized that they had left the city and were riding on the highway. Someone said,

"The first turn to the left is Krzemionki, the killing grounds."

Through an opening in the torn tarpaulin he looked out. An early morning fog covered the fields. They'll kill us before the sun rises, he thought.

In a moment yellow road signs loomed out of the fog, and he just had time to hiss, "Now, a crossroads . . ."

They froze; they held their breath. The truck slowed down, listed to one side, and made a sharp right turn. The road sign said: Auschwitz. Someone grabbed his hand; he heard muffled sobbing. In the pale film of light he caught sight of a young, boyish face. Von Galoshinsky was crying.

THE
PIG

The man was hiding in a barn. He was no longer young, and he had been through a lot. He had been hiding behind a straw partition for two weeks. It wasn't much of a shelter. Nor was this his first hiding place. For weeks he had wandered in and out of attics, barns, cellars, even family graveyards, all bought dearly, with cash. Each day and night of those weeks could fill a book, if only the pen could take on this burden of despair and helpless loneliness.

But he was alive. By now, the nearby town in which he had been born and which he knew as well as his own face, was half dead, gutted by *Sonderkommandos*. The area had been reduced to a few inhabited buildings; the doors of the other houses had been sealed, and through the windows you could see bedding, pots, and clothing strewn about the floor.

It was a glorious summer, sweltering, auguring a good harvest. But it was stuffy in the hayloft; dust from the dry straw floated in the air of these few square meters. The man made a small chink for himself in the outside wall of the barn; through this chink he could keep an eye on a scrap of the world: the meadow in front of the peasant's fenced-in yard and a strip of road. The house was right next to the main road that linked the small town with the county seat of T———. He spent entire days at the chink in the wall. He took turns and looked first with one eye, then with the other. He witnessed fragments of daily events: the peasant's wife walked past, a cart drove by, a child fell down.

He couldn't smoke because of the danger of fire. So that chink kept him going. At least he could see.

He had already pondered his entire life; for hours at a time he held imaginary conversations; he recited Latin texts that he had to struggle to recall; he was close to developing a split personality, which he diagnosed with a doctor's objectivity. He listened attentively to shots from the town; he listened attentively to the silence. Then he counted. He counted the steps of people walking around the farmyard, the blows of the ax when they chopped wood. What kept him alive in this attic was the chink. He saw.

That day he was awakened by the sound of motors. It was gray outside and he couldn't see very much. But he knew it was the sound of trucks driving from T——— to the town. He recognized the big trucks by their heavy rumbling. He dropped onto the floorboards and after a while he could no longer hear the rumbling diesel engines, his heart was beating so loudly. He knew what they signified; he thought about how the last time, when he was still in the town, twenty trucks packed solid had driven out of there. "They're coming back for the rest of the living," he whispered to himself, "for the rest of the living."

Silence soon fell over the outskirts of town and dawn broke slowly. The yellow flowers on the meadow, whose names he could not recall, shone in the sunshine. He kept his eyes glued to that little bit of highway visible through the chink, although nothing was happening there. For the moment nothing was happening there.

Then he placed his ear against the crack and listened. After an hour that seemed to him like a century he heard a distant scream. He swayed and shut his eyes, but closing his eyes didn't save him. He saw everything with the precise, experienced eyes of a witness to four actions, all of which, by some miracle, he had survived intact.

The screams were growing in intensity, or perhaps it only seemed that way to him. Still, the shots could not be a hallucination. Dulled by a distance of two kilometers, they came one after the other, chaotically, from several directions. He cowered in a corner with his hands over his eyes. Whom had they taken? Whom were they torturing? He knew them all, he had treated them.

Suddenly he shook off his weakness and pressed himself against the chink. They were returning. Impulsively he jabbed his finger into the opening to make it larger; now he could see clearly.

The meadow beside the highways was crowded with gaping onlookers. He even recognized the children of the peasant couple who were hiding him. They stood there, full of curiosity, looking towards the town, from which the rumbling trucks straining uphill could be heard.

"I can't," he said, and slumped into a corner, but he stood up again and watched without blinking.

He saw the first two trucks clearly. It seemed to him that he recognized a woman, the one standing at the back with her arms hanging limply at her sides. But the third truck he saw as if through a mist. No one screamed, no one shouted, no one wailed.

He had counted six trucks when suddenly he heard an inhuman shriek. He froze. A commotion rippled through the crowd; everyone swarmed to the roadway.

What had happened? Had someone tried to escape? But

the trucks didn't stop nor were there any shots. The rumbling of the motors was drowned out by the wailing of the spectators. The crowd broke up and angrily dispersed, loudly discussing what had happened.

He could barely contain himself until his peasant arrived that evening; he was trembling with excitement.

"What happened?"

"What happened was . . . ," the peasant responded in his singsong Volhynian accent, "the devil take them! They ran over a pig!"

That evening he did not touch his food, that night he didn't close his eyes.

There was one more attic, then a forest; he endured the last months of the war buried in a hole beneath a pigsty. The woman was poor but she gave him food, protected him, and when he was very ill, she swore from the goodness of her heart that she would bury him under the most beautiful apple tree in her orchard. It was at her place that he survived the war. When she pulled him—filthy, covered with lice, unable to walk—from his underground hiding place, he said, "You know, when they ran over that pig, I didn't believe there were any human beings left . . ."

"Yes, yes," she answered him, as if talking to a child. And being a sober, sensible woman, she thought to herself, "The poor thing has gone crazy from happiness. He's babbling about pigs!"

TITINA

Perhaps because Ludek was the youngest, the commandant ordered him, "Bring Titina." That's all, he didn't give him a list like he gave the others who had just left the *Judenrat* building and scattered through the town. Ludek asked, "By myself?" but the short, bald commandant didn't answer and slammed the door in his face. A storm of voices was raging behind the door.

It was a warm, windy night. The ice was breaking up on the river, and the sound of the water could be heard everywhere in town. There wasn't a single light in the houses, just thick darkness, sleep.

He walked quickly. The river's voice grew stronger. Titina lived next to the bridge. "Good evening," he imagined himself saying, and heard Titina answer, *"Bonsoir, jeune homme."*

"Bonsoir, Madame," he corrected himself—she insisted he speak to her only in French. The little desk under the window, the worn volume from Larousse, the gilded binding of *Letters from My Windmill*. And the smell of mold from the dark room. Even back then she showed signs of becoming a madwoman. That mustiness. She never opened the windows. Dark, slender spruce trees outside. She referred to her little house as "Spruce Manor," and rolled her *r*'s as befits a teacher of French.

"Comment va ta maman?"

"Merci, elle va bien."

His mother in her nightgown, her wrinkled neck, her slack, goose-bump skin. She hadn't even had the time to dress.

"Ludek, they've sent for you." And she began to weep, "My child . . ."

He dressed efficiently—trousers, tunic, the cap with the shiny visor. "Mama, where's my truncheon?"

"I'll ask the Marciniaks, you can hide in their barn."

A month before, she was crying because the *Judenrat* didn't want him. She walked kilometers, tried all her connections, spent hours cooling her heels in the corridor outside the *Judenrat* president's door. "I want to save you," she used to say.

"Don't be hysterical, Mama."

She raised her hands to her neck as if to choke herself. That was her strongest gesture of despair; it was what she kept doing the night they took his father away.

"I didn't know. I didn't expect . . . ," she could hardly talk. She grabbed his arm. He freed himself gently but firmly.

"Stop it, Mama, I have to go," he said.

She wanted to embrace him, but he stopped her with a look, although he knew what that embrace was supposed to mean. She was asking for his forgiveness.

"Elle ne va pas bien."

Dear Zofia, *la belle Sophie*, and her little boy! Titina's voice is low and hoarse, like that of a sorceress. Her long dress shimmers and rustles; on her nails is a gleaming, blood-red shell.

"I don't want a candy, no!"

"He'll get used to it," says the hoarse voice of the sorceress, and his mother laughs lightheartedly.

"Why don't you air out your house, Titina?"

A scream came from the direction of Castle Hill. He stopped and listened. Silence now, nothing, only the sound of the river. The river and his own heart. "She's half mad, or maybe by now she's gone completely mad," he said out loud. Again he stopped. No, he wasn't mistaken. The center of town was already awake. Someone was running, someone screamed once, then again; someone kept shouting and shouting. He took off his cap, bared his head to the wind. Spring was in the air. If I don't do it they'll throw me out. From the other end of town, near the railway station, came the sound of motors. They'll drive by the bathhouse and wait there. How many trucks? Six? Five? How many names were on the list? Old people, cripples, madmen. How many people did they want? He leaned over the bridge railing. One thrust of his body and he would be floating away, carried along by the current into the heart of that roar. "Ludek, take care of Mama, be brave and obedient." What does brave and obedient mean? To shift his center of gravity a centimeter beyond the bridge railing and let his hands hang over? To get crazy Titina? To float away with the river?

Suddenly he saw them coming. So that's what it looks like. Completely normal. They're walking, leading the others by the arm. So silently. Jozek's broad shoulders, Heniek's boyish silhouette, and between them two bags of bones. A man gets smaller in old age. They stopped. Jozek was so angry he could barely speak:

"So, you're admiring the landscape, mama's boy? Let us do all the work, right? You scum! You heard them—if something goes wrong, then two of *us* will have to go. And it won't be me, that's for sure."

One bag of bones is a man, the other a woman. He drew back to let them pass. The woman took tiny steps, bent over as if she might fall any minute. Her eyes were closed.

Titina's house was behind the garden; the spruce trees came right up to the porch. He had a hard time opening the gate; it was frozen solid. He sank up to his knees in snow. It probably hadn't been shoveled since the start of winter. He turned on his flashlight: there weren't any footsteps. Had she not left the house all winter? Maybe she was dead. God, let her be dead. A white snowy porridge had drifted over the rotted steps; three steps, he still remembered that. The spruce trees had grown as high as the roof.

He pushed the door with his shoulder. It gave way; there was no key in the lock. The entranceway, the familiar damp odor of mold.

"Don't be afraid," Mama had said, "she's a little strange, an eccentric old maid, but she knows the language so well, she lived in Paris for many years. Now she's old and very poor."

"And loony." He smiled.

"Shush, Ludeczek, please. Don't act so badly brought up. 'Strange' is what I said. Bow to her politely."

He wanted to shout, but could only manage a sharp whisper. "Miss Titina!" I'm hoarse, he thought.

He shouldn't have called out "Titina." That wasn't her real name, only a nickname; probably no one even knew what her real name was. But the commandant had also said it: "Bring Titina." He remembered that when he began to study French he asked his mother where she had gotten such a funny name, and his mother sang him the song "Titina, oh Titina, Let's play the concertina." The gay melody flew out of his mother's lips like a swift little bird, and his mother, with her head cocked to one side, looked like a comic little bird with a round neck. Then she told him a long story about a ball, a complicated story which she must have found amusing because she kept stopping to laugh, and his father became angry at her for telling such nonsense to a child. He was seven then; his mother thought it the proper age for studying foreign languages. It was then, at the ball that Mother had described, that the name Titina stuck forever to the queer, old woman whom he now had to lead to the square in front of the bathhouse.

His whisper got no response. He felt for the light switch; it sparked once, but the house stayed dark. He forgot about his flashlight, and with his arms outstretched, walked to the end of the hall where, just as he remembered, double doors led into the big dark room.

He stopped in front of the doors and pressed his ear against them. There was a ringing silence, which turned into the ringing of a church clock striking eleven. There was one hour left.

He waited until the final, eleventh chime faded away. He thought, she's probably dead, I'll go back, I'll say she's no longer alive. There are no footprints in the snow and the door is locked.

But he remained there with his ear to the door and now it was neither the silence nor the clock that rang, but his own heart ringing inside him, sounding an alarm.

"Miss Titina," he said once more, cajolingly. He was begging her: don't be alive.

"Who's there?"

He was horrified and jumped back.

"*Entrez,*" said the low, hoarse voice that he recognized immediately.

He entered.

She was sitting up in bed, barricaded behind a pile of pillows. All he could see was her head with its straggly gray hair sticking straight up like wires. She was holding a candlestick in her raised hand.

As he approached, his shadow suddenly leapt onto the wall beside the shadow of her medusa head and then slowly, steadily covered it.

The face that peered out from the bedding was huge, mottled with liver spots. "A wreck," he thought aloud, and repeated with a strange satisfaction, "a wreck, a wreck."

She was watching him closely. He sensed that she was struggling to remember him. He felt a cramp in his stomach, a quiver of nausea, and undid the collar of his tunic.

"Please get up," he said. "All Jews have to be at the *Judenrat* now."

She didn't move. A slight tremor passed across her face and she smiled.

"You're probably here for a lesson."

"No. You have to get up. I'll take you to the *Judenrat*. Everyone . . ."

"Unfortunately, I'm not giving lessons at the moment."

He bent over her and, fighting nausea, said sharply, "Please get up."

I can't do it, they'll throw me out, he thought. She won't

go, I won't be able to make her go. If only I had someone to help me.

"Get up!" he shouted.

She dropped the candlestick on the floor. He picked up the candle and kicked a pot away with his foot. Bread crusts, hard as bone, scattered all over the floor. He gathered them up carefully.

"What a way to speak to me!" said Titina. "And whom do I have the pleasure? ..."

He didn't answer. Once more he repeated, calmly, and now politely, "Please get up and get dressed. I shall be escorting you to the *Judenrat*. All Jews have to assemble at the *Judenrat*."

"*Tiens, tiens.*" She twisted her head. "To the *Judenrat*? I've never had anything to do with the *Judenrat*. And I don't want to have anything to do with them. *Voilà*, young man. And now you may leave."

"Miss Titina!" he screamed. "The Germans ordered ..."

"*Les sales boches!*"

"I'll help you."

Her shapeless bag of a face was up against his; her eyes were swimming with tears. She grabbed his hand. "Whose son are you, child?" she asked. And without waiting for an answer she whispered, "Son . . . you are the son of . . ."

"Of Zofia," he answered obediently, despite himself.

"*Mon Dieu*, Zofia's son—*la belle Sophie*! How could I . . . I knew you would come. Why haven't you come for so long? Do you have your notebook and grammar?"

"Miss Titina, you have to come with me. The Germans have ordered . . ."

"I remember, I was at a ball with your mother, ah . . .

she was the only one who remembered that a lonely woman needs some diversion. The garrison commander danced the mazurka with me. *Mon Dieu*, so she hasn't forgotten about me. Sit down at the desk, open your notebook. *Elle était si belle, ta maman . . .*"

He sat down. He was very tired. Titina's hoarse voice reached him from far away. He was thinking: What am I doing here? Why? And also: It would be so nice to fall asleep and wake up when all this is over. All what? All this.

His mother used to run from the president to the secretary, from the secretary to the vice president, and return home weak, broken, ill. He noticed her stockings had holes in them. People are ungrateful, she said. They owe your father so much and now, when they've killed him, no one will help me. They say that you're too young. She cried in front of him. Until one day she returned home a different, a much younger, woman.

"Ludeczek, you won't go to the camp!" she called out. "They agreed, they swore to me!"

He was neither happy nor sad. "And what will I do, Mama?" he asked.

"What do you mean, what? You will be an orderly. That's a good post." Everyone said "post" now. He didn't like that word—orderly! And tonight she was choking herself again.

The heavy fall of the church bell. He jumped up as if he'd been scalded.

"It's been years since anyone has come, I've been alone for years. They all forgot . . . not a single lesson . . ."

This madwoman keeps going around in circles, he thought in a rage.

"No one, no one . . ."

"But now they've remembered you," he suddenly heard his own voice, his own unrecognizable voice, and he noticed that these words got through to her.

"They've remembered," he repeated louder and more emphatically. And with a growing fury such as he had never felt before, he added, "The commandant wants to study French with you."

Having said this, he backed away. His heart was pounding, in his throat. But it was too late now.

Titina straightened up, with more strength than he had expected.

"*Monsieur le commandant veut prendre des leçons chez moi?*"

"Yes! Now, at once," he screamed.

You scum, he said to himself. You filthy scum.

The loading was finished now, the square was empty, the snow trampled flat. The SS were standing near the trucks; a group of policemen, with their bald-headed commanding officer, were off to one side.

At the sight of Ludek leading the bizarre figure dressed in a long coat and a hat festooned with flowers, the SS roared with laughter. One of them pointed his riding crop at the steps which led up into a truck and graciously extended his hand to Titina.

"*Merci, Monsieur,*" she said before she disappeared into the dark interior of the truck filled with stale human breath.

The bald man handed Ludek a flask and told him, "Take a drink, it'll make you feel good." Ludek obediently pressed it to his lips and gulped it like water. He felt as if he were on fire.

He flung the flask onto the ground and took off running. He ran blindly through the empty town, and then across the fields, he ran sinking into the drifts of snow, he kept falling and getting up and running towards the ever closer, ever more threatening roar of the river.

NIGHT

OF

SURRENDER

I met Mike in a park, in a pretty little town on the Alsatian border. I had been imprisoned there briefly in 1943, which was complicated, considering that I was a Jew using Aryan papers. Now the war was ending, the front was falling apart around Stuttgart, and the surrender was expected any day.

Mike was a very nice fellow, and in those first days of freedom I was feeling very lonely and sad. I used to go to the park every day. It was immaculately kept and the rhododendrons were in full bloom, covered with pale violet flowers. I would walk to the park, sit on a bench, and tell myself that I should be happy to have survived, but I wasn't happy, and I was upset to be so sad. I went there every day and the girls from the camp figured that I had met a boy; they were envious and curious. Their suspicions were confirmed on the day Mike walked me back to the camp; and from then on he would come to get me every day at four and we would go for a stroll.

Michael was very tall, he had funny long legs, his uniform trousers fit tightly, his waist was as slender as a girl's. He wore large eyeglasses with rectangular frames. He smiled like a child, and if he wasn't so big, you could have mistaken him for a teenager; but he was a serious grown man, a professor of mathematics, already twenty-seven, ten years older than I.

He would take my hand—my head came up to his elbow —and we would go strolling in the park or along the Rhine, and he would always whistle the same tune. Much later, I found out that it was Smetana's *Moldau*, but at that time I didn't know its name or who had composed it. My knowledge of the world and of life was one-sided: I knew death, terror, cunning, how to lie and trick, but nothing about music or poetry or love.

This is how I met him: One day I was sitting on the bench beside the pale violet rhododendrons. It was evening and I should have gotten up and returned to the camp for supper, but I kept on sitting there, I didn't feel like getting up even though I was hungry, and I didn't notice the lanky boy with the glasses and the American uniform who had sat down on the edge of the bench. When he asked, "What are you thinking about?" I was terrified, and he burst out laughing.

I answered in my broken English, "I was in a German prison here,"—though I hadn't been thinking of that at all, only about supper, because I was hungry.

"Did they beat you?"

"No."

He looked closely at me, then said, "That's funny."

I didn't know what was funny—the fact that I had been in prison or that they hadn't beaten me. Some kind of moron, I thought, but he kept on asking me questions.

"And why did the Germans lock you up in prison?"

I looked at him as if he were a creature from another world.

"Don't worry. I just wanted to know what it was like for you."

He looked at me seriously, and his eyes shone with a warm, golden light. Maybe he's not such a fool, I thought. But watch out, I told myself, wait a bit. You held out for so many years, you can hold out for another week or two. The war is still going on.

But already I anticipated the enormous relief it would be to say those three words—their weight was growing more unbearable each day. I smiled faintly, and in that teary voice befitting the revelation of one's life story, said: "Ah, my history is very sad, why return to those matters? I don't want to."

"Poor child!" He stroked my hair and took some chocolate out of his pocket. "But you will tell me some day, won't you?"

It was milk chocolate. I love milk chocolate; it's light and melts in your mouth. The last time I ate chocolate was before the war, but I didn't say anything, I just got up to go to supper—the potatoes and canned meat in gravy we got every day.

The next afternoon Mike brought me some enormous, dark violets, and I rewarded him with the life story I had patched together over the last three years; it moved him as it was meant to. I was sorry that I was still lying, but consoled myself with the fact that the true story would have been a hundred times more horrifying.

The girls from the camp were jealous, and in the evening they would ask in detail about everything. After a week, they asked, "Has he kissed you?" and when I answered, "No," they were very disappointed. And that was the truth. Mike brought me more chocolate (because I had told him, after all, that not since before the war . . .). He bought me ice cream, he held my hand, and sometimes, when we lay near the Rhine, he stroked my hair and said it was silken and shiny. He also told me about his home and the school where he taught, and about the garden he worked himself. It all sounded like a fairy tale from a storybook for well-brought-up children, and sometimes I smiled to myself, especially when he talked about flowers and mowed grass. I never asked him if he had a girlfriend in America. It was obvious that he did, but he never mentioned her.

Sometimes we didn't say anything. The water in the Rhine glittered like fish scales, the weeds flowered in the ruins, airplanes circled overhead and they too were silvery and long, like fish. But there was no reason to fear them, and now, without getting that tightness in your throat, you could watch them dive, grow huge, and mark the earth with the shadow of a cold black cross.

"Ann," Mike would say, giving my name, Anna, its English form, "isn't this nice?"

"Very nice," I would answer, and he would say, "Very, very nice, my dear," but it wasn't very nice at all and it couldn't be very nice as long as I was lying to him.

That day, when we were returned from the park, the rhododendrons were already yellow and withered. Mike asked, "Why won't you tell me everything about yourself? It would make you feel better."

I was well trained. I replied instantly, "But I told you."

"Not everything, Ann. I'm sure that was only a part, maybe not even the most important part. Why don't you trust me?"

Again he had that warm, golden glow in his eyes, and I thought: I am mean and nasty.

"The war taught all of you not to trust anyone. I'm not

surprised. But listen, the war is over. You have to learn to believe in people, in happiness and goodness."

"You're talking like a professor, and a stupid one. You think everything can change just like that? Believe in people? It makes me laugh"—I wanted to say throw up—"when I hear such idiotic stuff."

"Ann, I want to ask you something."

My heart began to pound, because that was what everyone said before they asked, "Are you a Jew?"

"Well, ask," I said, but he didn't say anything; he just looked at me and I couldn't help seeing the tenderness and concern in his glance. I felt like touching his face, pressing close to him, asking him not to go away, telling him that I didn't want to be alone anymore, that I was tired of standing outside myself and watching every move.

"Well, ask. I'm waiting," I said.

We were standing at the gate to the camp. It was suppertime. A crowd of DPs with aluminum mess kits for their potatoes and canned meat with gravy were crossing the large square where, every morning, roll call and edifying prayers were held.

I looked at Mike and noticed that a muscle in his right cheek was quivering.

"Would you go away with me?"

"With you? Well . . . where?" I asked only to gain time and calm down. I knew very well what he meant.

"Where? Where? To the moon!" All at once, he grew serious. "You know what I'm asking and you know that I mean it. I've thought about it for a long time and I've come to the conclusion that it's very nice for us both when we're together. Right?"

"You're saying this out of pity, aren't you?" I laughed.

"A poor victim of the war, she lost her parents in the uprising, she's all alone in the world."

"Stop it, that's horrible. You know that isn't true. It's not pity, I just want things to be nice for us. I know that together . . . Don't answer now. Think about it. I'll come tomorrow. You can tell me then. We've known each other for almost a month, and I want you to stay with me. But Ann," he didn't let go of my hand, "get rid of all those defenses. Trust me. I want to bring you up all over again, teach you to live again."

For the first time he looked like a serious, grown-up man.

"All right, Professor," I said, and then ran away. The next day the surrender came and everyone was going wild. I waited for Mike for a whole hour on the low wall in front of the camp. By the time he arrived that evening, I had lost hope. Lying on my bunk in the empty room—all the girls had gone to a party—I thought, with the army you never can tell, they might have transferred him suddenly, and goodbye! I lay there dazed, trying to recall the melody he always whistled, and which I still didn't know the name of. But I couldn't, so I tried to summon up his smile and his long funny legs. When he walked into the room, I was very happy—but only for the second it took me to remember that today I had to tell him everything. Though I very much wanted to be rid of the burden of those three words, I was frightened. Mike seemed like a total stranger. But that feeling, too, lasted only a moment, because he said, "My God, you look like a schoolgirl, like a child, and I'm an old man." He began singing to that *Moldau* melody, "Such an old man, but so very much in love," and we laughed till tears came to our eyes. Only on the way to the Rhine did I remember the gnawing fear inside me and though the night was quite warm, I felt cold.

The river no longer looked like a silver scale; it was dark and the water babbled against the shore. From the direction of town came songs, shouts, the noise of fireworks.

I thought, what a shame to ruin this night. We should be drinking and celebrating like normal people.

"Ann," Mike said softly, "today is doubly important. Right? The war has ended and we are beginning a new life. The two of us. I know your answer; I can read it in your eyes. I know—you'll stay with me."

He kissed me tenderly on the mouth; his lips were soft and gentle.

"Michael," I said, "before I tell you I'll stay with you, you have to know the truth about me. You have to know who I am."

"Do you think I don't know? You're a small, lost child of the war. You're seventeen years old, but you're just a little girl who needs protection and tenderness."

I looked at the sky. A rain of man-made stars showered down, falling like fiery fountains. The water in the river was sparkling with color, the ruins of the town were colored, the whole night was colored.

"Michael." I looked into his eyes. Now I couldn't afford to miss even the tremor of an eyelid. "I am Jewish."

Perhaps it was because I was hearing those words for the first time in three years, those words I had carried inside myself constantly, or because none of the things I had feared registered on Mike's face, but I felt tears well up, and I opened my eyes wide so as not to burst out crying.

"And that's what you were hiding from me so carefully? Whatever for?"

I spoke quickly, feeling lighter with every word.

"You don't know, and you can't know. You don't know what it means to say, 'I am Jewish.' For three years I heard those words day and night but never, not even when I was alone, did I dare to say them aloud. Three years ago I swore that until the war ended no one would hear them from me. Do you know what it means to live in fear, lying, never speaking your own language, or thinking with your own brain, or looking with your own eyes? Michael, it's not true that my parents died in the uprising. They were killed right in front of me. I was hiding in the wardrobe that the Germans forgot—just think, they forgot!—to open. You don't know what an action means. You don't know anything, and I won't tell you. When I came out of the wardrobe, I found my parents' bodies on the floor. I ran out of the house. I left them there just as they were, it was night, deathly still. I ran to the village where friends of my father lived and they gave me their daughter Anna's birth certificate. I got on the train and got off in a big city, but there was a round-up in the station—you don't even know what a round-up is!—and they shipped me directly to Germany to do forced labor. I was lucky, very few people had such good luck, because others saw their parents' bodies and then were tortured and killed. But I milked cows, mowed grass, knew how to lie, to invent stories at the drop of a hat. I was lucky, no one found me out, and except for the few days spent in prison, I lived in peace until the end of the war. But at night I dreamed all the time that I was hiding in a wardrobe and was afraid to come out. But I don't want to tell you about it, why did I tell you? Tonight is such a joyous night, and I've ruined it completely."

His kind eyes were so sad. He didn't stop stroking my hand and I didn't want him to stop. I longed to go to sleep, I felt as if I had been in labor, with its healthy pain and healthy exhaustion.

"What's your real name?" he asked.

"Klara."

"Klara," he repeated. "Clear one . . . but you'll always be Ann to me."

The sky above us was golden and red. We could hear the noise of the rockets, and red stars were falling into the river. I bowed my head and heard that wondrous music: the beating of a human heart.

"I will do everything to make you forget that nightmare. And you will forget," Mike said after a moment. "You're very young. You'll see, time will cover over all this the way grass grows over the earth. But promise me one thing: that you will remain Ann—and not just in name. It will be better that way, believe me."

I felt a chill down to my fingertips.

"For whom?" I asked clearly, because suddenly it seemed to me that the river was making a lot of noise and that my words were drowning in that noise.

"For you, for us. The world is so strange, Ann, it will be better if no one other than me knows about Klara."

"Michael, *you too?*"

"Oh, you child, it's not a question of anti-Semitism. I have no prejudices, it'll simply be easier that way. You'll avoid a lot of problems, it'll be simpler for you to cast off the burden of your experiences. You've suffered so much already! I'm not saying this out of prejudice, but for your own good. And since you've already left it behind . . ."

The river was still roaring, the river that was flowing inside me.

"If you don't want to I won't insist. You can decide for yourself, but believe me, I have experience, it'll be easier for you this way."

He touched his lips to my hair; in the glare of the rocket exploding into light above us I saw the anxiety in his eyes. I felt cold and once again I didn't know how to cry.

"Let's not talk about this now, it's not important," he pleaded. "Not tonight, the night of the surrender . . ."

He didn't finish. He wasn't stupid.

I silently shook my head. Maybe he didn't notice, maybe he didn't understand.

The water in the river was burning with the fire of victory and in the pure air of the May night we could clearly hear the singing that welcomed the end of the war.

THE
TENTH
MAN

The first to come back was Chaim the carpenter. He turned up one evening from the direction of the river and the woods; no one knew where he had been or with whom. Those who saw him walking along the riverbank didn't recognize him at first. How could they? He used to be tall and broad-shouldered; now he was shrunken and withered, his clothes were ragged, and, most important, he had no face. It was completely overgrown with a matted black thicket of hair. It's hard to say how they recognized him. They watched him from above, from the cliff above the river, watched him plod along until, nearing the first houses of the lower town, he stopped and began to sing. First they thought he had gone mad, but then one of the smarter ones guessed that it was not a song, but a Jewish prayer with a plaintive melody, like the songs that could be heard on Friday evenings in the old days, coming from the hundred-year-old synagogue, which the Germans had burned down. The synagogue was in the lower town; the whole lower town had always been Jewish—before the Germans came and during the occupation—and no one knew what it would be like, now that the Jews were gone. Chaim the carpenter was the first to come back.

A dark cloud from the burnt-out fire still lingered over the town, the stench still hung in the air, and gray clouds floated over the marketplace the Germans had burned.

In the evening, when the news had spread, a crowd gathered in front of Chaim's house. Some came to welcome him, others to watch, still others to see if it was true that someone had survived. The carpenter was sitting on the front steps in front of his house; the door of the house was nailed shut. He didn't respond to questions or greetings. Later, people said that his eyes had glittered emptily in the forest of his face, as if he were blind. He sat and stared straight ahead. A woman placed a bowl of potatoes in front of him, and in the morning she took it away untouched.

Four days later the next one came back. He was a tenant on a neighboring farm and had survived in the forest with the help of the farm manager. The manager brought the tenant back by wagon, in broad daylight. The old man was propped up, half reclining, on bundles of straw. His face, unlike the carpenter's, was as white as a communion wafer, which struck everyone as strange for a man who had lived so long in the open.

When the tenant got down from the wagon he swayed and fell face down on the ground, which people ascribed more to emotion than to weakness. In fact, it was possible to think he was kissing the threshold of his house, thanking God for saving him. The manager helped him up, and supporting him on his arm, led him into the entrance hall.

A week passed and no one came back. The town waited anxiously; people came up with all sorts of conjectures and calculations. The stench of burnt objects faded into the wind and the days became clear. Spring blossomed suddenly as befitted the first spring of freedom. The trees put forth buds. The storks returned.

Ten days later three more men came back: a dry goods merchant and two grain dealers. The arrival of the merchant upset the conjectures and calculations, since everyone knew that he had been taken away to the place from which there was no return. He looked just as he had before the war; he might even have put on some weight. When questioned, he smiled and explained patiently that he had jumped out of a transport to Belzec and hidden in a village. Who had hidden him, and in what village, he didn't want to say. He had the same smile on his face that he used to have before the war when he stood behind his counter and sold cretonnes and percales. That smile never left his face, and it astonished everyone, because no one from this man's family had survived.

For three days the grain dealers slept like logs. They lay on the floor near their door, which was left slightly ajar, as if sleep had felled them the moment they walked in. Their high-topped boots were caked with dried mud, their faces were swollen. The neighbors heard them screaming in their sleep at night.

The grain dealers were still sleeping when the first woman returned. No one recognized her. Only when she reached the teacher's house and burst out sobbing did they understand that she was his wife. Even then, they didn't recognize her, so convincing was her beggar woman's disguise. She had begged in front of Catholic and Orthodox churches, had wandered from church fair to church fair and market to market, reading people's palms. Those were her hiding places. From beneath her plaid kerchief peered the drawn face of a peasant woman.

They asked in amazement: "Is it you?"

"It's me," she answered in her low voice. Only her voice was unchanged.

So there were six of them. The days passed, the gardens grew thick and green. They're being careful, people said, they're waiting for the front to move—it had been still for so long that an offensive seemed likely. But even when the offensive began and the front made a sudden jump to the west, only a few more came back.

A wagon brought the doctor back. He had lain for nine months in a hole underneath the cowshed of one of his patients, a peasant woman. He was still unable to walk. The accountant and his son and the barber and his wife returned from a bunker in the forest. The barber, who had once been known for his mane of red hair, was bald as a bowling ball.

Every day at dusk, the dry goods merchant left his house and walked towards the railway station. When asked where he was going, he explained, "My wife is coming back today." The trains were still not running.

The farmer, a pious man, spent more and more time by his window; he would stand there for hours on end. He was looking for a tenth man, so that the prayers for the murdered might be said as soon as possible in the ruins of the synagogue.

The days kept passing, fragrant and bright. The trains began to run. The people in the town no longer conjectured and calculated. The farmer's face, white as a communion wafer, shone less often in his window.

Only the dry goods merchant—he never stopped haunting the railway station. He would stand there patiently, smiling. After a while, no one noticed him anymore.

CRAZY

. . . everybody thinks I'm crazy, but I'm not. I know—every crazy person says that, but really, there's nothing wrong with my head. If only God *would* make me crazy! It's my heart that's sick, not my head, and there's no cure for that.

You can see, I have crooked legs and a hump. I'm four feet eleven inches. I have a face that frightens children. But my children were such good children, and every morning and every evening they would kiss me on both cheeks and say, "Good morning, Papa. Good night, Papa."

Doctor, have you heard people say that beautiful children are born to ugly people? Have you? My children were *beautiful*! They had blond hair like silk, and straight legs, plump as sausages. My wife, who was a good woman, my wife and I used to say, "God is just; He has given the children what we don't have any of." There were three of them, all girls. The oldest was seven and the youngest three.

I'm a garbageman. I swept the streets. There was plenty to sweep and it was a hard way to earn my bread, Doctor, breathing in that stench. After work, in the bathhouse, I could never wash myself clean enough. In that bathhouse! My oldest girl was already going to school and she brought home a report card—all A's from top to bottom. Sometimes in school they would shout at her, "Your father's a garbage-man," but she . . . a heart of gold . . . such a child! Can you understand, Doctor? No, it's impossible.

Later I swept the ghetto; at least it was called sweeping.

But who worried about garbage? I had a broom and I walked around with that broom. The children were hungry, and as I walked around, sometimes something would turn up. Sometimes someone gave me something . . .

The younger ones didn't understand, but the oldest . . . a golden child. It was still "Good morning" every day, "Good night" every evening. I used to tell her, "Sleep peacefully." Peacefully!

When the first action was organized everyone said they would take me, because they took cripples, and I'm a dwarf with a hump. I hid on the roof. During the second action we ran away to the woods. When the third action happened, I was walking down the street with my broom, because I used to start work at five in the morning, and the action began at five-thirty. Do you know what those brooms are like? They're made out of twigs, long and thick. Do you see how tall I am? Four feet eleven inches.

When the trucks drove into the square in front of the bathhouse, I squatted in a corner between two houses, and the broom hid me. No one, not the SS nor the *Ordnungsdienst*, suspected there was anyone there, they only saw a broom. I was shaking so hard that the broom was swaying. I heard everything, because they locked them up in the bathhouse till they loaded them on the trucks. I was saying: O God, O God, O God. I didn't know myself what I wanted of God. Did I even know if there was a God? How could I?

Someone was running, trying to escape, and he touched the broom with his hand. It fell down and now if someone had looked at that corner it would have been the end of me. I was afraid to pick it up, because they were already leading them to the trucks.

Doctor! My children were on the first truck, my three

girls. I saw that the oldest understood, but the others were crying from plain fright. Suddenly they stopped crying and the youngest, the three-year-old, cried out, "Papa! Papa, come to us!"

They saw me. They were the only ones who saw me in that corner.

Doctor! So what did I do? Their father, I came out, ran over to them, and together we . . . right?

No. I put my finger to my lips and shook my head at them, they shouldn't cry out, they should be quiet. Sha!

The two youngest called to me again, but that one, my firstborn, she covered their mouths with her hand. Then they were quiet . . .

Now please give me a certificate that says I am not crazy, or they'll throw me out of work and lock me up in a hospital. Better yet, give me some medicine so I won't have to hide and shout, "I'm coming! I'm coming!" because in any case they can't hear me anymore.

JUMP!

Anka used to come with her parents, in a pink dress and gleaming patent leather shoes. The adults would drink tea in the parlor, while we children went out to the garden, and there the persecution of the small, well-dressed guest would begin.

It would start quite innocently with an ordinary game of "school," which we played by throwing a ball against the wall of the house and performing a series of pirouettes, turns, and hand clappings before we caught the ball again. The wall was covered with dark stains, the plaster was scaly and peeling; those were the results of our strenuous practice sessions, through which we had achieved perfection.

But she—perhaps she wasn't allowed to damage the walls of her house, perhaps she didn't like this game—she always "flunked out" in the first round, and then, impeccably pink, would stand politely under a tree and watch us clap our hands, whirl, and bounce a white tennis ball under our bent knees. Easily, without "flunking," we moved from one round to the next, until we reached the height of success— "graduation."

"We" were Elzbieta and I, and our friend Tadeusz, who had taught us this new expression "flunked out" when his brother failed his high-school graduation exam.

After we'd finished we would ask her, "Would you like to start over?" Well-mannered, she nodded silently, though intimidated by our circus performances, and obligingly took the ball, which would bounce into the tangle of raspberry bushes during the first difficult trick. When the winner ended the game of "school" by acquiring the title of "triple-professor," it would be time for mumblety-peg.

"You have to be careful," we warned her every time, "it's a dangerous game." Tadeusz would lift the bottom of his shorts to reveal the thick, ugly caterpillar on his thigh, a scar from a recklessly thrown pocketknife.

"When they sewed up his leg he squealed like a pig," we'd tell her proudly.

Turning pale, she would reluctantly take hold of the rusty knife. I don't know what frightened her more—the ugly caterpillar on Tadeusz's thigh or having to eat grass, which was the penalty for losing. She would welcome the end of the visit and leave with her parents, clean and fragrant as always. We would hang on the fence, watching them. When they disappeared around the bend in the street, Tadeusz would spit out the word that both Elzbieta and I feared like fire: "Sissy!"

That is how I remember her from those days. And the two Ankas—one pink, with a bow in her hair, the other unconscious, dying in the hut of a Ukrainian deacon—refuse to be reconciled in my mind, even though time brought all of us something quite different than what our childhoods promised.

Back then, as a child, she was pretty, and later she became even prettier, with a flawless, classical beauty. By that time the ball and the pocketknife were things of the past, and a high swing had been hung in the garden.

Only Anka's face was beautiful, but its loveliness made up for her somewhat heavy figure and her legs, which

Tadeusz once said were Jewish legs because they were red. Tadeusz had whispered that to Elzbieta and then to me, and we had immediately checked our own legs to see if he was right. Our legs were burnt brown by the sun and were covered with scratches and scabs, without a trace of red.

"That's because you're not real Jews," he explained. "Real Jews are scared, and you're not afraid to jump off the swing. You're not real and that's why your legs aren't red."

We were sitting on the grass and Anka was standing near the swing; it was her turn. She stood there and looked towards the house, listening for the voice that would herald the end of her visit—her reprieve.

"Climb up," we told her, "and bend your knees. It's easy."

We were playing "douse the candles." Chandeliers of blooming lilac grew around the swing, and you had to make the swing go as high as you could and then spit down onto them. After this came the dramatic finish, a big jump into the soft, fluffy grass.

It was a good swing, all you had to do was pump your legs gently and it would pick up speed and sail way up over the barn roof, over the lilac chandeliers, which you were supposed to extinguish.

The swing posts creaked. "Bend your knees," we shouted. "Don't be afraid, bend your knees!"

Flying high in the air, she looked like a beautiful doll. The wind billowed the pink sail of her dress, revealing the red pillars of her legs in all their splendor. She was already high above the lilacs. We waited for her to spit.

"She's dried up out of fear," Tadeusz said contemptuously.

"Jump!" we shouted. "Jump now!"

Her lovely face turned to stone. Many years later, she jumped.

After the war, I heard what had happened to her and her parents. I could visualize their destiny as if it were sketched out before me. At first it looked so serene, even lazy, like the surface of our river, unbroken by waves. Then suddenly it began churning, and caught in a whirlpool, it plunged into the abyss. There was nothing exceptional in this sudden convulsion of fate that trapped one in a fatal whirlpool. Nevertheless, this pattern, almost like a geometric drawing, had never seemed so clear to me until I learned about Anka.

At first, her fate promised to be as serene as her beauty. School went by without any triumphs but also without any failures, and was followed by an early, prosperous marriage. She had already begun to resemble her mother, and would surely have relived her mother's life—a fine home in a small town, pretty children, pretty dresses, the annual trip to a health resort—if the sentence of time hadn't made tragic heroes even of those least suited to play the part.

I last saw her when things were still relatively peaceful. She was strolling through town with her husband; they were walking arm in arm, stately and dignified. Her face was still beautiful, though no longer quite so perfect; perhaps this new, almost imperceptible flaw was the mark of time, which disfigured the less perfect of us so much more brutally. She was wearing pink. Maybe it was this gay, childish color, or the fact that, at the time, even eighteen-year-olds were nostalgic for the past. In any case, I said to her, "Do you remember 'douse the candles'?"

She looked at me in amazement. She did not remember.

And shortly after that, she descended into hell. In whispers, frightened by the import of their words, people talked about how she became a widow. The story was told in detail; it had happened out in the open, in public. There were people who saw and heard how the SS-man directing the action from in front of the *Judenrat* building took out an index card and read off the name. They saw how her father, a member of the *Judenrat*, looked thunderstruck. It was his son-in-law's name.

They saw him walk off, stop for a moment, move his arms in a nervous gesture, walk and stop, walk and stop. But he kept on walking.

There were no witnesses, however, to the scene in their home, to his knocking at the entrance to the hiding-place, to his calling out his son-in-law's name, telling him to come out. There are no witnesses because all of them were killed.

Everyone saw the two men returning. They walked side by side, without speaking.

How did she live under the same roof with her father after that? Did they look each other in the eye? What did they say? I don't know. Some questions should not even be thought. The facts alone suffice.

They weren't together for long. She fled to a different city, and a month later people heard that she had been deported to Belzec. Soon after that her parents were killed.

But not her. Anka did not die in Belzec.

Did someone in that train racing through the forest shout, "Jump! Jump now!"?

Surely someone must have shouted; one person after another jumped. She jumped into the darkness. All this is known because a young Ukrainian deacon found her at the edge of the forest, helpless, half-conscious. She lay in his hut. He said that she was beautiful, that he wanted to save her. He called a doctor, bought medicine for her, prayed to his God. But fate wouldn't listen. She died several weeks later without regaining consciousness.

THE
OTHER
SHORE

I looked up and saw that someone was approaching. It annoyed me. I wanted to get up and leave, but I was too lazy. I searched through my purse for my glasses. It was a woman—small, frail, elderly. She walked slowly, stepping carefully, as if she were walking on glass. But the path that led down to the pond was a good one—soft and loamy even during hot dry spells. I know that, because every summer I spend a few days in Z—— with friends, who own a cottage there and a magnificent wild orchard. We pick fruit and tend the overgrown flower beds. It's a long way from their house to the pond. You have to go through the village, then down the road to the very last farm and only then turn right, down a wide path lined with poplars. The path leads to the edge of the pond, where there are two flat tree stumps. Farther along, there are rushes and reeds, and no way to cut through.

She was coming towards me, no doubt heading for the other stump. And I had had such high hopes for this evening! There are thoughts that wither under the gaze of others, that are wounded by the breath of others, that the slightest disruption destroys. I saw the woman as my enemy. As she got closer, I could see her more clearly; she wasn't so small or so old. She was no more than forty, with a gentle, kind face. But she was still walking strangely, haltingly. When she emerged from the trees she stopped briefly, hesitated. Only then did she wade into the grass, lifting her legs high, as if she were being stung by nettles. But there weren't any nettles.

She's certainly timid, I thought. A moment ago I was ready to drive off the enemy, but now I could hardly repress a friendly hello. But she wasn't looking my way; I don't think she even saw me.

She walked up to the edge of the pond. The water there was muddy, but a dozen or so meters out, it suddenly grew clear, pure blue. The pond was oval, egg-shaped, overgrown with reeds, and not at all picturesque. But it was fragrant with sweet flag. She stood there for a long time, scanning the water; it puzzled me. What was she looking for?

I sat down and watched her. She was just a few steps away from me, delicate, meticulously dressed. And yet . . .

It was some time before she slowly and gracefully turned her head. She met my gaze without the least bit of surprise. So she had known that I was there. She said, "It's a beautiful warm evening."

And I had been thinking God knows what! I felt bad and answered her with a smile, "It's pleasant by the pond."

"Except for the mosquitoes. There's an awful lot of them."

We both reached for our cigarettes at the same moment. I gave her a light, she sat down next to me, on the other stump. We smoked in silence. The sun went down, and mist rose from the water.

"This is the first time I've been here since that day," she

said suddenly. She seemed amazed at her own words and at herself for saying them. "That's why I was so . . . so . . . ," she groped for the right word. "That's why I didn't acknowledge you. There was no one here then."

So I was right! I kept silent. It didn't matter what I said or if I said anything at all. Unasked, uninvited, she was going to tell me everything—to me, an absolute stranger, on the first meeting. One pebble had fallen; I awaited the avalanche.

"I wasn't brave enough. I was afraid to come, and whenever the day approached, I looked for obstacles, arguments to prove I didn't have to. Only this year was different. At the beginning of the month I said to myself, you have to paint the apartment and a trip costs money. Except that I didn't want to paint the apartment, I wanted to come. I wanted to see . . ."

She looked at me.

"Am I boring you?"

I shook my head no. She seemed pleased and went on.

"It was today, exactly. The same day, the same time. I didn't have a watch then, but the sun had already gone down and it was chilly, like it is now. See that little house? The last one on the road? That's where I was hiding with a friend of the family. It was near the end. They had already shot my sons and my husband. I remember that people were saying, 'How can she do it? Why should she save herself? For whom?' But you know, the life force has such strong roots, you can't tear it out. Even after those we love most have died. But you are young, what do you know about that?

"I was living with them in a room, not in the cellar, in a regular room. It was small and dark, but it had a bed. A bed and a chair. At night I would sit on the bed, because

I couldn't sleep, and during the day, on the chair. I patched sacks, I sewed, I had to do something. One idle moment and I would have gone mad. Even I wondered, why are you sitting here? For whom? But I kept on sitting. There were only women in the house: the grandmother, the mother, two daughters. Men would sometimes drop by at night, stay for a day or two, and disappear. I knew something was up but I didn't want to ask.

"One day I was sitting in the chair darning stockings when the grandmother came in. She was shaking, and my first thought was that someone had betrayed us. I knew what the penalty was. But all she said was, 'Paula, you have to run away. There's going to be a search here. My daughter's husband has been caught. And he wasn't the only one. They're looking for my son, too. They could be here any minute. When it quiets down you'll come back.'

"She spoke as if I were a child; once upon a time she had been my teacher. I suddenly felt like a schoolgirl, and I said, 'What a misfortune. Of course, I'm on my way.' Perhaps I even curtsied, I don't know. Anything was possible then.

"Where should I go? I thought. The ghetto no longer existed, the city was *judenrein*. It wasn't even my city. I had no friends here, no one, not a soul. I was penniless. As soon as I left—out the window, straight out into the garden —I realized that, with all that sitting, I had forgotten how to walk. My joints had grown rusty. Did you see how I was walking? Like a stork.

"Their garden was full of beautiful flowers I had never seen in the city. My eyes ached from so much color. And the orchard! I would gladly have stayed in the orchard. It had been a long time since I had seen trees, grass, but I couldn't, because of the owner.

"So I set out on the road, that one over there." She pointed with her hand. "It was straight and white and flat as an ironed ribbon. The road was wide but I felt as if I were walking a tightrope. I turned right, away from town. I was looking for a forest to hide in. It must have been far off, maybe in the other direction. I couldn't see it. With every step—and I'd only taken a few—I felt wearier. It wasn't the physical effort, it was everything. Again I asked myself: For whom? Why? My strength had left me. Those roots, you know, those roots, they suddenly tore loose.

"When I saw the poplars, and then the thicket and the reeds, I thought to myself: that way. I'd heard them mention this pond—the children were forbidden to come here unsupervised. So I knew that that was where I must go. And all at once I grew calm. It was the right road.

"I walked slowly, still looking. It was pretty here, green, though not quite the same green as today. Paler, dusty, it hadn't rained for weeks.

"I passed these stumps and entered the water right here. Just as I was; I didn't even take off my shoes. It was warm, murky, dirty. I thought: What good luck that I didn't meet anyone, that I can do this peacefully, alone. I walked out farther and farther, deeper and deeper. I began to think about my children and my husband and about how much crueler their end had been than mine. Dusk was falling, it was warm and quiet, and I was peaceful and calm.

"The water was already up to my waist, then higher. The bottom dropped off very gently. It was difficult to walk. My legs kept sinking into the muck and I had to keep pulling them out. I said to myself, one more step, one more, there, in the center it's deep. Sweat was pouring down my face, this slow dying was so hard. Then the water grew cold and transparent. I saw that I was almost there. I moved faster,

I was rushing now. I couldn't catch my breath, there was a roaring in my ears. I was afraid I wouldn't have the strength to get to the place where the ground would slip out from under my feet. I raised my head to catch my breath and then . . . Do you know what happened then? Right in front of me—distinct, nearby—I saw the other shore. The pond was shallow. It was normally shallow, and now with the drought and no rainfall . . . I collapsed on the ground, exhausted, wet . . . alive."

I thought she would keep talking, but she was silent, staring at the other shore, and her face, shadowed by twilight, was still gentle and kind.

"Thank you," she said after a moment.

I wanted to ask her what happened next, but I knew she wouldn't say more. The deepening twilight revealed the stars. A late bird took flight from a branch and flew low over the water, rippling the surface with its wings.

SPLINTER

The girl touched his arm with her hand, her delicate, manicured hand, blossoming with polished pink nails.

She said, "Let's not talk about that any more. You promised."

They were walking along a steep road in the hills of a defeated country, in a region unscathed by war, clean and radiant. The meadows with their lush, long, unmown grass looked especially lovely—bright with flowers and alive with the chirping of crickets. Summer had come unusually early this year. It was only the beginning of June and already the air was heavy with the smell of the lindens.

They were both very young and they were going on a picnic. When she asked him to stop talking, the boy fell silent in embarrassment. He smiled sheepishly and said, "Look, I've got to tell everything to the end. And since I don't have anyone but you . . . It's like a deep splinter that has to be removed so it won't fester. Do you understand?"

"I understand, I understand, only you can't talk about it all the time, without stopping. You haven't stopped for"— she hesitated, they had known each other scarcely a week— "*days*. It's for your sake that I want you to stop. But if you think it helps to . . ."

She raised her beautiful hands in a gesture of helplessness. She was giving in.

"It's beautiful here," said the boy. "This picnic was a good idea. Your idea. You always have the good ideas, I'm still not much good for anything."

"Don't worry. At first I used to think pretty clothes would never make me happy again." She laughed. She was wearing a bright print dress flowered like the meadow.

"You! You were lucky. You spent the whole time in the country, you fed chickens. Come on, don't get angry, that's really terrific luck, and that's why you're so lovely and calm and why I need you. You have such beautiful legs! I'd like to paint them someday. I always wanted to paint. Always, before the war, that is. But I was thirteen then."

The sun was setting when they entered the dense forest; the pine trees stood in rows like soldiers. The soft needles gave way beneath their feet.

"Speaking of good ideas," said the girl, "let's go to the movies tonight. Or to a dance. Okay?"

The boy bent down, picked up a pine cone, sniffed it. "Let's take a little rest," he said.

They lay down on their backs and looked up at the pure, pale blue sky suspended over the woods.

"My mother would be very happy," he began. His eyes were closed, his long lashes emphasized his pallor. He waited a moment, but the girl did not ask why. So he went on:

"She would have been very happy to know that I am lying here in the woods with a girl I love, that I'm lying around on such a splendidly happy day, with nothing threatening me. Because she was probably thinking of that when . . ."

Again he fell silent. The girl lay motionless with her hands under her head and gnawed on a blade of grass.

"What happened with my mother was the worst thing possible," he said after a moment. "Worse than the bunker in the forest where I ate leaves and roots for a week—remember I told you?—worse than a beating in the camp. You have hands just like my mother's. She was very beautiful. We were living in a small, dirty room. Father was already in the camp, and we had nothing to eat. But my mother was still beautiful and cheerful and never showed any fear in my presence. I was terribly afraid. She was, too, I knew it, her quiet crying would often wake me up at night, but I would lie still as a mouse so she could cry in private. Before what I am about to tell you happened, my mother was crying less often at night, because we were supposed to get papers and cross to the other side. Now I couldn't fall asleep, I was so worried about whether our papers would arrive in time. She was calm; she taught me different prayers and how to cross myself, and carols, because it was almost Christmas.

"I didn't sleep *that* night either. I heard them come through the gate, but I was speechless with terror. I lay there stupefied, I couldn't even call out 'Mama.' I heard wailing from the ground floor; they were beating people. I didn't scream until they were walking up the stairs. Those stairs used to creak, I can still hear them creaking, it's funny, isn't it?"

He paused, listening intently. The wind was blowing and several pine cones fell from the trees. It was hot, as before a storm.

"How did she do it? It was unbelievable—it took her just a few seconds. Later I often thought that she must have rehearsed that moment beforehand, she acted so quickly and efficiently. She jumped out of bed, scooped up the bedding in one motion and stuffed it into the bureau drawer; in a second she had folded up her cot and slipped it behind the wardrobe. Then she grabbed my hand and shoved me into the corner by the door, and before they could pound on it, she opened it wide and hospitably. The heavy oak door pressed me against the wall and hid me. There was only one bed and one person in the room. I heard her ask in German, "What's the matter?" Her voice was so calm she could have been speaking to the mailman. They struck her in the face and ordered her, just as she was, in her nightgown, to go downstairs."

He took a deep breath. "That's almost all there is to say. Almost . . . Because you know, when my mother pressed me against the wall with the door, I grabbed the handle and held on to it, even though it wouldn't have shut on its own, since it was a heavy door and the floor was uneven."

The boy fell silent; he brushed away a bee. Then he added, "I would give a great deal to let go of that handle . . . . ," and then, with a smile that begged forgiveness, he added, "You'll have to have a lot of patience with me. All right?"

He turned over lazily and looked at her face. The girl was gorgeous, slightly pink. Her warm lips were parted, she was breathing calmly, evenly. She was asleep.

THE
SHELTER

That summer I happened to be traveling on a line I rarely take. It was a local route punctuated with frequent stops, and the passenger train lumbered slowly and noisily through the monotonous countryside. Occasionally it ran alongside a forest, but mostly it kept stopping at villages and small towns with unfamiliar names. After an hour of this, I was cursing my wretched plan for this trip. I felt filthy, black with soot, unkempt. I tried to sleep, I tried to read, I basked in the sunshine like a cat and tried to kill my boredom with cigarettes—a method as unhealthy as it was useless.

The train was empty. Practically no one was traveling in my direction except for peasant women in white kerchiefs with bulging baskets that smelled of the milk and sour cream they were carrying to market. They got on at one station only to get off at the next. In the corridor several men were arguing loudly about the Sunday soccer game; it seems it was all the goalie's fault. The conductor was dozing.

We were stopped at one of those tiny stations—two posts and a board with some writing on it, evidently the name of a village some distance from the track—when I saw a man and a woman boarding the train. In the city, I wouldn't have noticed them, but there, in that open field . . . The woman was beautiful, carefully groomed, dressed in a simple but elegant suit and narrow, flat-heeled shoes that fit her feet like second skins. The man was somewhat older, graying at the temples, tall, thin, with strong features. His raincoat was slung carelessly over his arm. They had an overnight bag and a huge, soft-sided suitcase.

I looked out the window: nothing, only oats, rye, clover, a narrow road through the fields, along which a wagon, on its way back from the station, trailed behind it a cloud of gray dust. They must have come in that wagon. From where? From whom? They had the air of people who had lived in the city for generations, and I would have bet anything that they were not returning from a visit to relatives.

They entered my compartment. The man lifted their baggage onto the luggage rack and helped the woman off with her jacket. In her blouse she looked younger, more girlish, though its whiteness emphasized her eyes, which were red from crying. She sat down in the corner, away from the window, although the window seat was free. She took the man's hand with a fearful gesture as if seeking his support. But what kind of support could he give her? The cigarette in his hand was trembling.

The train made a gentle arc; small houses scattered beside the river suddenly appeared and just as suddenly disappeared behind dark clouds of trees.

"Shh, shh," I heard him whisper. Turning, I saw that the woman was crying. She cried softly, silently, the tears flowing down her cheeks in thin rivulets. It was a pitiful kind of weeping, and the man kept repeating "hush, hush" as if he were comforting a child. But suddenly he glanced in my direction, bent over the weeping woman, and whispered distinctly, "Stop that now."

She couldn't stop. She was crying loudly, hiding her face in her hands.

"A temporary indisposition," her husband explained. "It will pass in a moment."

"Lie down, dear." By now his voice had taken on a slightly impatient tone; the word "dear" had an edge. "Why don't you just laugh it off?"

"Laugh?" she cried out.

There was a deep, raw bitterness in her cry, and I thought: It's not a laughing matter. She's right. I stood up; they should be left alone. I took my suitcase down from the rack and was about to leave, when he spoke to me.

"No, please stay. It will be easier if we're not alone."

I felt stupid. I didn't know what to do. I reached for my book but he, clearly dreading silence, immediately said, "May I ask what you are reading?"

I told him the title. Of course he knew it. "It's about the occupation, isn't it?" he asked. Now they both burst out laughing, and even though it was an uneasy laughter, I still could not hide my amazement.

"They warped people. Why waste words on it?" he said at last. "Where were you?"

"In a camp."

"We were in hiding. Not far from here, in the village where we got on the train."

"Yes," I said, "I understand. It's hard enough just returning to those years in memory, not to mention going back . . . I understand your being so upset."

Suddenly the woman's voice rang out. "That's not it! You're mistaken."

She began her story. A week ago they received a letter from their aunt and uncle, inviting them to come to a name day party and see their new home. The aunt and uncle—she didn't use any other name for them—were the people who had hidden them in 1943. They had come upon them quite by chance. After weeks of wandering in the forest, when they no longer had any rusks or onions in their knapsacks, when their legs were swollen, and autumn had blown away all the berries, they knocked at the door of the first hut on the edge of the woods.

It was evening, and a good-looking, youngish woman was bustling around inside. "What do you want?" she asked.

They didn't know how to answer. Was it only bread they were asking for?

"Aha, so that's it." She took a better look at them. They looked like wild animals. "Where are you from?"

They didn't answer. A pot of milk was on the stove. They looked at the milk. Heavy and big-boned, she walked up to them, and still eyeing them suspiciously, she gave them some milk. They lapped up the milk like dogs. Then she told them to go.

They just stood there, so she repeated, "And now get out of here fast, before someone sees you."

She was chasing them out, but they stood there rooted to the spot.

The train screeched, braking, and the woman fell silent. Her husband wiped his sweaty forehead, stood up, closed the window, and then opened it again. The voices of the people boarding the train drifted in from the corridor. A man with a child in his arms opened the compartment door and backed out, saying, "Ugh, it stinks of smoke in here, this is not for us."

"All aboard!" yelled the conductor. A bridge rattled under the wheels, the little town outside was silent and dead. A moment later we entered the forest.

"We couldn't leave," the woman continued. "The warmth made us tired, we longed to sleep. I thought, she's good, she gave us milk. So when she came closer, angry and impatient, ready to shove us out the door, I grasped her hands and begged her shamelessly. I felt her dry, strong fingers in my hands, roughened from the brambles in the forest, and I pleaded with her the way a believer pleads with God. Her fingers grew limp; it was her heart softening. She opened the door to a small room and said, 'Wait here till my husband comes home.'

"We collapsed onto our knapsacks. That same night Olek had a long talk with the husband. The money we had was only enough to feed two people for two or three months—really almost nothing. But we promised to pay the cost of a new house—if we survived. Their hut was dilapidated, and you could smell poverty in every corner. They took us in. We cried like children; it was the first night we'd spent under a roof in many weeks.

The next night the husband began building a shelter. As a young man he had been a mason, so the work went quickly. It was a bricked-in storage area in the cellar, so narrow it could scarley hold two people. But we went down there only as a last resort, when a visitor came, or when there were Germans in the village. Otherwise, we sat in the small room during the day, and at night when the doors were locked, in the main room of the hut. Olek played cards with the husband, and we read books aloud.

"But towards the end of the war, when troops were quartered in the area, we didn't leave our shelter for two months. Those two months were very hard. I had pains in my joints; but being sick was the least of it. It was impossible to lie down. We had to sit all the time. We played 'geography'—all the rivers that begin with *A*, the cities with *B*; we asked each other Latin words. Eventually, we didn't even feel like eating. We just sat there. Sometimes Germans spent the night in the hut. We could hear their footsteps; they would go down to the cellar, they were right there on the other side of the thin wall with potatoes piled against it. The day the couple came downstairs and said it was over, I couldn't even rejoice. We were ill for a long time afterwards, seriously ill, it seems, because the husband, who came to visit us in the hospital, looked at Olek and said, 'That's the end of my house.'

"Afterwards we started all over from the beginning. We had only the clothes on our backs, and if it were not for my husband . . ."

"What of it?" the husband interrupted. "I began to work, and slowly, slowly things fell into place. I sent the first money we saved up to Aunt and Uncle; we sent money every month, for three years. They came to visit us. Why not? We were all alone, no one in our families survived; so they became like . . .

"They finished building the new house in the spring—three rooms and a kitchen. They asked us to come and see it, but somehow it turned out that either I had to work, or my wife was sick, always those joints. A week ago we got a letter; they were inviting us to Uncle's name day party in their new home."

He took a deep breath, lit another cigarette. It was quiet for a moment. Had they not had the courage to go?

She was the first to break the silence.

"So we finally went. We were five years older. What am I saying? *Fifty* years older! I said to Olek, 'Look, that bridge, we slept here. Do you remember the town of W——? And the station at N——? We bought our tickets there and were afraid to get on the train. Just think,' I said to him, 'we are alive, we are together, nothing threatens us.' I was happy.

"I waved out the window to Uncle, who was waiting for us at the station. We climbed into his wagon, which was filled with straw. My heart was pounding. I waited for the hut and the garden to appear around the turn. I forgot that a new house would be standing there. It was pretty—but seeing that hut would have touched my soul. The house? It looked just like any other house. With a red roof. His wife stood in the doorway, dressed in her holiday clothes, and though I smiled and kissed her, I felt bad because I missed the old hut. They asked us in. It was clean, the red floors were newly waxed, there were cretonne curtains on the windows. The table was set with cold meats and vodka. Olek knew right away what was bothering me and said quietly, 'Don't get hysterical,' but out loud he exclaimed over how nicely they had furnished it. Uncle poured out the vodka, he wanted to make a toast, but his wife said, 'No, first take a look around.'

"We began in the kitchen, then we went into the living room, the bedroom, and another room for the son who had returned from the army. We thought they had shown us everything, but then they said, 'And we kept you in mind, too. Here, take a look!'

"The husband pushed aside a wardrobe and I looked— a white, blank wall. But when he went down and touched the floor, I grabbed Olek's hand. I didn't see anything yet, but that gesture was familiar.

"He lifted a red, waxed board and told us to look closely. 'There, now, just in case something happens, you won't have to roost like chickens, a shelter as pretty as a picture, with all the comforts!'

"I leaned over and saw stairs leading down into a small, dark room, without any windows or doors. It had two beds, two chairs, and a table."

The train shook as it switched tracks and picked up speed. We were approaching the city. The sky had turned pale, and the little houses on the outskirts appeared outside the windows, behind low, evenly trimmed hedges.

"What are we supposed to make of that?" asked the man. "Sentenced to a hiding-place, sentenced to death once again? And by whom? By good people who wish us well. It's appalling. To build a hiding-place out of the goodness of one's heart! That's what's so horrible. There, in that house, it was as if I were kneeling above my own grave."

"Horrible," I repeated. I said something else about how the war twisted people, and I felt ashamed; it was so banal, so polite. But they didn't hear me. They were hurrying towards the exit, and their quick, nervous steps gave the impression of flight.

TRACES

Yes, of course she recognizes it. Why shouldn't she? That was their last ghetto.

The photograph, a copy of a clumsy amateur snapshot, is blurred. There's a lot of white in it; that's snow. The picture was taken in February. The snow is high, piled up in deep drifts. In the foreground are traces of footprints; along the edges, two rows of wooden stalls. That is all. Yes. This is where they lived. She recognizes those stalls; they used to be market stalls and were converted to living quarters. Well, perhaps she has put it badly, they were simply enclosures made with boards.

There were about a dozen of those stalls, on both sides of the narrow market street. Three or four families lived in each stall. The loose-fitting boards gave no protection from rain or snow.

"That's the ghetto," she says again, bending over the photograph. Her voice sounds amazed.

Of course she is amazed. How did they survive there? Such . . . such, well, it's hard to express. But in those days no one was surprised at anything.

"They did such terrible things to us that no one was surprised at anything," she says out loud, as if she has just now understood.

The person who took the photograph must have been standing next to the building in which the *Judenrat* was housed. That was an actual house, not a stall. Three windows in front, and an attic under the roof.

She pushes the photograph away. "I prefer not to be reminded . . ."

"So, in the last stage, the ghetto was reduced to this one little street?"

Yes, of course. It was a tiny street, Miesna, or Meat, Street. There used to be butcher shops in those stalls and that's why, at the end, the ghetto was called "the butcher shop ghetto."

How many people were there? Not many. Maybe eighty. Maybe less.

Again she reaches for the photograph, raises it to her nearsighted eyes, looks at it for a long time, and says, "You can still see the traces of footprints." And a moment later, "That's very strange."

That's the direction they walked in. From the *Judenrat* down Miesna Street. She looks at the footprints, the snow, and the stalls once again.

"I wonder who photographed it? And when? Probably right afterwards: the footprints are clear here, but when they shot them in the afternoon it was snowing again."

The people are gone—their footprints remain. Very strange.

"They didn't take them straight to the fields, but first to the Gestapo. No one knows why, apparently those were the orders. They stood in the courtyard until the children were brought."

She breaks off: "I prefer not to remember . . ." But suddenly she changes her mind and asks that what she is going to say be written down and preserved forever, because she wants a trace to remain.

"What children? What trace?"

A trace of those children. And only she can leave that trace, because she alone survived. So she will tell about the children who were hidden in the attic of the *Judenrat*, which was strictly forbidden under pain of death, because children no longer had the right to live. There were eight of them, the oldest might have been seven or so, although no one knew for sure, because when they brought them over they didn't look at all like children, only like . . . ach . . .

The first tears, instantly restrained.

They heard the rumbling, a horse cart drove up to the yard, and on it were the children. They were sitting on straw, one beside the other. They looked like little gray mice. The SS-man who brought them jumped down from the cart, and said kindly, "Well, dear children, now each of you go and run to your parents."

But none of the children moved. They sat there motionless and looked straight ahead. Then the SS-man took the first child and said, "Show me your mother and father."

But the child was silent. So he took the other children one by one and shouted at them to point out their parents, but they were all silent.

"So I wanted some trace of them to be left behind."

In a calm voice she asks for a short break. With an indulgent smile she rejects the glass of water they hand her. After the break she will tell how they were all shot.

THE
TABLE

A PLAY FOR
FOUR VOICES
AND BASSO
OSTINATO

CHARACTERS:

FIRST MAN, 50 years old
FIRST WOMAN, 45 years old
SECOND MAN, 60 years old
SECOND WOMAN, 38 years old
PROSECUTOR, 35–40 years old

The stage is empty and dark. Spotlights only on the witness, seated in a chair, and the prosecutor, seated at a desk.

PROSECUTOR: Have you recovered, Mr. Grumbach? Can we go on? Where did we stop? . . . Oh, yes. So you remember precisely that there was a table there.

FIRST MAN: Yes. A small table.

PROSECUTOR: A *small* table? How small? How many people could sit at a table that size?

FIRST MAN: Do I know? It's hard for me to say now.

PROSECUTOR: How long was it? A meter? Eighty centimeters? Fifty centimeters?

FIRST MAN: A table. A regular table—not too small, not too big. It's been so many years . . . And at a time like that, who was thinking about a table?

PROSECUTOR: Yes, of course, I understand. But you have to understand me, too, Mr. Grumbach: every detail is crucial. You must understand that it's for a good purpose that I'm tormenting you with such details.

FIRST MAN: (*resigned*) All right, let it be eighty centimeters. Maybe ninety.

PROSECUTOR: Where did that table—that small table—stand? On the right side or the left side of the marketplace as you face the town hall?

FIRST MAN: On the left. Yes.

PROSECUTOR: Are you certain?

FIRST MAN: Yes . . . I saw them carry it out.

PROSECUTOR: That means that at the moment you arrived at the marketplace the table was not there yet.

FIRST MAN: No . . . Or maybe it was. You know, I don't remember. Maybe I saw them carrying it from one place to another. But is it so important if they were bringing it out or just moving it?

PROSECUTOR: Please concentrate.

FIRST MAN: How many years has it been? Twenty-five? And you want me to remember such details? I haven't thought about that table once in twenty-five years.

PROSECUTOR: And yet today, while you were telling your story, on your own, without prompting, you said, "He was sitting at a table." Please concentrate and tell me what you saw as you entered the square.

FIRST MAN: What did I see? I was coming from Rozana Street, from the opposite direction, because Rozana is on the other side of the market. I was struck by the silence. That was my first thought: so many people, and so quiet. I noticed a group of people I knew; among them was the druggist, Mr. Weidel, and I asked Weidel, "What do you think, Doctor, what will they do with us?" And he answered me, "My dear Mr. Grumbach . . ."

PROSECUTOR: You already mentioned that, please stick to the point. What did you see in the square?

FIRST MAN: The square was black with people.

PROSECUTOR: Earlier you said that the people assembled in the marketplace where standing at the rear of the square, facing the town hall, and that there was an empty space between the people and the town hall.

FIRST MAN: That's right.

PROSECUTOR: In other words, to say, "The square was black with people," is not completely accurate. That empty space was, shall we say, white—especially since, as you've mentioned, fresh snow had fallen during the night.

FIRST MAN: Yes, that's right.

PROSECUTOR: Now please think, Mr. Grumbach. Did you notice anything or anyone in that empty white space?

FIRST MAN: Kiper was sitting in a chair and striking his boots with a riding crop.

PROSECUTOR: I would like to call your attention to the fact that none of the witnesses until now has mentioned that Kiper was walking around with a riding crop. Are you certain that Kiper was striking his boots with a riding crop.

FIRST MAN: Maybe it was a stick or a branch. In any case, he was striking his boots—*that* I remember. Sometimes you remember such tiny details. Hamke and Bondke were standing next to him, smoking cigarettes. There were policemen and Ukrainians standing all around the square —a lot of them, one next to the other.

PROSECUTOR: Yes, we know that already. So, you remember that Kiper was sitting in a chair.

FIRST MAN: Absolutely.

PROSECUTOR: So if there was a chair in the marketplace, wouldn't there have been a table as well?

FIRST MAN: A table . . . just a minute . . . a table . . . no. Because that chair seemed so . . . wait a minute . . . No, there wasn't any table there. But they carried out a small table later. Now I remember exactly. Two policemen brought a small table out from the town hall.

PROSECUTOR: (*relieved*) Well, something concrete at last. What time would that have been?

FIRST MAN: (*reproachfully*) Really, I . . .

PROSECUTOR: Please, think about it.

FIRST MAN: The time? . . . God knows. I have no idea. I left the house at 6:15, that I know. I stopped in at my aunt's on Poprzeczna Street, that took ten minutes, then I walked down Miodna, Krotka, Okolna, and Mickiewicza streets. On Mickiewicza I hid for a few minutes inside the gate of one of the houses because I heard shots. It must have taken me about half an hour to walk there.

PROSECUTOR: How much time elapsed from the moment you arrived in the square to the moment when you noticed the policemen carrying the table out from the town hall?

FIRST MAN: Not a long time. Let's say half an hour.

PROSECUTOR: In other words, the policemen carried a table into the marketplace around 7:15. A small table.

FIRST MAN: That's right. Now I recall that Kiper pointed with his riding crop to the place where they were supposed to set the table down.

PROSECUTOR: Please indicate on the map you drew for us the exact place where the policemen set the table down. With a cross or a circle. Thank you. (*satisfied*) Excellent. Kiper is sitting in a chair, the policemen carry in the table, the length of the table is about eighty centimeters. How was the table placed? I mean, in front of Kiper? Next to him?

FIRST MAN: I don't know. That I couldn't see.

PROSECUTOR: If you could see them carrying in the table you could see that, too—perhaps you just don't remember. But maybe you can remember where Kiper sat? At the table? Beside it? In front of it?

FIRST MAN: Obviously, at the table. When someone waits for a table, it's so he can sit at it. He was sitting at the table. Of course. That's what people do.

PROSECUTOR: Alone?

FIRST MAN: In the beginning? I don't know. I wasn't looking that way the whole time. But later—this I know—

they were all there: Kiper, Hamke, Bondke, Rossel, Kuntz, and Wittelmann.

PROSECUTOR: (*slowly*) Kiper, Hamke, Bondke, Rossel, Kuntz, and Wittelmann. When you testified a year ago you didn't mention either Rossel or Wittelmann.

FIRST MAN: I must have forgotten about them then. Now I remember that they were there, too.

PROSECUTOR: Were they all sitting at the table?

FIRST MAN: No. Not all of them. Some of them were standing next to it.

PROSECUTOR: Who was sitting?

FIRST MAN: What I saw was that Kiper, Hamke, Bondke, and Kuntz were sitting. The rest were standing. There were more than a dozen of them, I don't remember all the names.

PROSECUTOR: How were they seated, one beside the other?

FIRST MAN: Yes.

PROSECUTOR: Is it possible that four grown men could sit one beside the other at a table that is eighty centimeters long?

FIRST MAN: I don't know. Maybe the table was longer than that; or maybe it wasn't big enough for all of them. In any event, they were sitting in a row.

PROSECUTOR: Who read the names from the list?

FIRST MAN: Hamke or Bondke.

PROSECUTOR: How did they do it?

FIRST MAN: People walked up to the table, showed their *Arbeitskarten*, and Kiper looked them over and pointed either to the right or to the left. The people who had good

Arbeitskarten went to the right, and those whose work wasn't considered important, or who didn't have any *Arbeitskarten*, they went to the left.

PROSECUTOR: Was Kiper the one who conducted the selection?

FIRST MAN: Yes. I'm positive about that.

PROSECUTOR: Did Kiper stay in that spot during the whole time the names were read? Or did he get up from the table?

FIRST MAN: I don't know. Maybe he got up. I wasn't looking at him every minute. It took a very long time. And anyway, is it that important?

PROSECUTOR: I'm sorry to be tormenting you with these seemingly unimportant details . . . In other words, is it possible that Kiper got up and walked away from the table, or even left the square?

FIRST MAN: I can't give a definite answer. I wasn't watching Kiper every minute. It's possible that he did get up from the table. That's not out of the question. Still, he was the one in charge at the marketplace. Kiper—and no one else. And he was the one who shot the mother and child.

PROSECUTOR: Did you see this with your own eyes?

FIRST MAN: Yes.

PROSECUTOR: Please describe the incident.

FIRST MAN: The woman wasn't from our town, so I don't know her name. She was young, she worked in the brickworks. She had a ten-year-old daughter, Mala. I remember the child's name; she was a pretty little girl. When this woman's name was called she walked up to the table with her daughter. She was holding the child by the hand. Kiper gave her back her *Arbeitskarte* and ordered her to go to the right. But he ordered the child to go to the left. The mother started begging him to leave the child with her, but he wouldn't agree. Then she placed her *Arbeitskarte* on the table and walked to the left side with the child. Kiper called her back and asked her if she knew the penalty for disobeying an order, and then he shot them—first the girl, and then the mother.

PROSECUTOR: Did you actually see Kiper shoot?

FIRST MAN: I saw the woman approach the table with the child. I saw them standing in front of Kiper. A moment later I heard two shots.

PROSECUTOR: Where were you standing at that moment? Please mark it on the map. With a cross or a circle. Thank you. So, you were standing near the pharmacy. How far was it from the table to the pharmacy?

FIRST MAN: Thirty meters, maybe fifty.

PROSECUTOR: Then you couldn't have heard the conversation between Kiper and the mother.

FIRST MAN: No, obviously. I didn't hear what they said, but I saw that the mother exchanged several sentences with Kiper. It was perfectly clear what they were talking about. Everyone understood what the mother was asking. Then I saw the mother place her *Arbeitskarte* on the table and go to the left with the child. I heard Kiper call her back. They went back.

PROSECUTOR: They went back and stood in front of the table, correct?

FIRST MAN: That's correct.

PROSECUTOR: In other words, they were blocking your view of the men who were sitting at the table, or at least of some of the men sitting at the table.

FIRST MAN: It's possible. I don't remember exactly. In any case, I saw them come back to the table, and a moment later there were two shots, and then I saw them lying on the ground. People who stood closer to them clearly heard Kiper ask her if she knew the penalty for disobeying an order.

PROSECUTOR: Was Kiper standing or sitting at that moment?

FIRST MAN: I don't remember.

PROSECUTOR: So, you didn't see him at the exact moment you heard the shots. Did you see a gun in his hand? What kind of gun? A pistol? A machine gun?

FIRST MAN: He must have shot them with a pistol. Those were pistol shots.

PROSECUTOR: Did you see a pistol in Kiper's hand?

FIRST MAN: No . . . perhaps the mother and child were blocking my view; or maybe I was looking at the victims and not at the murderer. I don't know. But in any case, I did see something that told me it was Kiper who shot them, and no one else.

PROSECUTOR: Namely?

FIRST MAN: Namely . . . immediately after the shots, when the mother and child were lying on the ground, I saw with my own eyes how Kiper rubbed his hands together with a disgusted gesture, as if to cleanse them of filth. I won't forget that gesture.

PROSECUTOR: (*summarizing*) And so, Mr. Grumbach, you saw Kiper sitting at a table in the company of Hamke, Bondke, Rossel, and Kuntz. Then you saw Kiper carrying out the selection and Kiper brushing off his hands immediately after you heard the shots that killed the mother and child. But you didn't see a gun in Kiper's hand nor the shooting itself. Is that correct?

FIRST MAN: Still, I assert with absolute confidence that the murderer of the mother and child was Kiper.

PROSECUTOR: Was Kiper sitting behind the table when your name was called?

FIRST MAN: (*hesitating*) I was one of the last to be called. My *Arbeitskarte* was taken and returned by Bondke. I don't remember if Kiper was present or not. By then I was already half dead.

PROSECUTOR: Of course. What time would it have been when your name was called?

FIRST MAN: What time? My God, I don't know, it was already past noon.

PROSECUTOR: Did you witness any other murders committed that day?

FIRST MAN: That day more than four hundred people were shot in the town. Another eight hundred at the cemetery.

PROSECUTOR: Did you see any member of the Gestapo shoot someone?

FIRST MAN: No.

PROSECUTOR: Were you one of the group that buried the victims in the cemetery?

FIRST MAN: No.

PROSECUTOR: Is there anything else that you would like to say in connection with that day?

FIRST MAN: Yes.

PROSECUTOR: Please, go ahead.

FIRST MAN: It was a sunny, cold day. There was snow in the streets. The snow was red.

FIRST WOMAN: It was a Sunday. I remember it perfectly. As I was walking to the square, the church bells were ringing. It was a Sunday. Black Sunday.

PROSECUTOR: Is that what the day was called afterwards?

FIRST WOMAN: Yes.

PROSECUTOR: Some of the witnesses have testified that the day was called Bloody Sunday.

FIRST WOMAN: (*dryly*) I should think the name would be unimportant. It was certainly bloody. Four hundred corpses on the streets of the town.

PROSECUTOR: How do you know the exact figure?

FIRST WOMAN: From those who buried the victims. The *Ordnungsdienst* did that. Later they told us, four hundred murdered in the town alone. A hard, packed snow lay on the streets; it was red with blood. The worst one was Kiper.

PROSECUTOR: Slow down. Please describe the events in the square as they occurred.

FIRST WOMAN: At six they ordered us to leave our houses and go to the marketplace. First I decided not to go, and I ran up to the attic. There was a window there, so I looked out. I saw people pouring down Rozana, Kwiatowa, Piekna, and Mickiewicza streets towards the square. Suddenly I noticed two SS entering the house next door. They stayed inside for a moment, then came out leading an elderly couple, the Weintals. Mrs. Weintal was crying. I saw that. They were elderly people. They owned a paper goods store. The SS-men ordered them to stand facing the wall of the house, and then they shot them.

PROSECUTOR: Do you know the names of the two SS-men?

FIRST WOMAN: No. One was tall and thin. He had a terrifying face. I might be able to recognize him in a photograph. You don't forget such a face. But they were local SS, because there were no outside SS in town that day. *They* did it, the locals. Four hundred murdered on the spot, twice that number in the cemetery.

PROSECUTOR: Let's take it slowly now. So, you saw two SS leading the Weintal couple out of the building and putting them against the wall. You lived on Kwiatowa Street. Was their house also located on Kwiatowa?

FIRST WOMAN: I lived on Kwiatowa at number 1; it was the corner building. The Weintals lived in a building on Rozana.

PROSECUTOR: What number?

FIRST WOMAN: I don't know, I don't remember . . .

PROSECUTOR: Did you see which of the two SS shot them? The tall one or the other one?

FIRST WOMAN: That I didn't see, because when they ordered them to stand facing the wall, I knew what would happen next and I couldn't watch. I was afraid. I moved away from the window. I was terribly afraid.

PROSECUTOR: Afterwards, did you see the Weintal couple lying on the ground dead?

FIRST WOMAN: They shot them from a distance of two meters; I assume they knew how to aim.

PROSECUTOR: Did you see the bodies afterwards?

FIRST WOMAN: No. I ran downstairs from the attic, I was afraid—with good reason—I was afraid that they would search the houses for people who were trying to hide, but I didn't go out into the street, I took the back exit to the garden and made my way to the marketplace by a roundabout route.

PROSECUTOR: Would you recognize those two SS in photos?

FIRST WOMAN: Perhaps. I'm fairly certain I could recognize the tall thin one. You don't forget such a face.

PROSECUTOR: Please look through this album. It contains photographs of members of the Gestapo who were in your town; but there are also photographs here of people who were never there.

FIRST WOMAN: (*she turns the pages; a pause*) Oh, that's him.

PROSECUTOR: Is that one of the men you saw from the window?

FIRST WOMAN: No, it's that awful murderer. It's Kiper. Yes, I remember, it's definitely him.

PROSECUTOR: Please look through all the photographs.

FIRST WOMAN: (*a pause*) No, I can't find that face. Unfortunately.

PROSECUTOR: You said "awful murderer". Did you ever witness a murder committed by Kiper?

FIRST WOMAN: (*laughs*) Witness? You're joking. The witnesses to his murders aren't alive.

PROSECUTOR: But there are people who saw him shoot.

FIRST WOMAN: I did, too. Sure—in the square, he fired into the crowd. Just like that.

PROSECUTOR: Do you know who he killed then?

FIRST WOMAN: I don't know. There were fifteen hundred of us in the square. But I saw him rushing around like a wild man and shooting. Not just him, others, too. Bendke, for example.

PROSECUTOR: When was that?

FIRST WOMAN: In the morning. Before the selection. But it's possible it also went on during the selection. I don't remember. I know that they fired into the crowd. Just like that.

PROSECUTOR: Who read the names from the list?

FIRST WOMAN: An SS-man. I don't know his name.

PROSECUTOR: How did they do it?

FIRST WOMAN: Very simply. Names were called out, some people went to the right and others to the left. The left meant death.

PROSECUTOR: Who conducted the selection?

FIRST WOMAN: They were all there: Kiper, Bendke, Hamm, Rosse.

PROSECUTOR: Which one of them reviewed the *Arbeitskarten?*

FIRST WOMAN: I don't remember.

PROSECUTOR: Who ordered you to go to the right? Kiper? Bendke? Hamm? Rosse?

FIRST WOMAN: I don't remember. At such a time, you know . . . at such a time, when you don't know . . . life or death . . . I didn't look at their faces. To me, they all had the same face. All of them! What difference does it make whether it was Kiper or Bendke or Hamm or Rosse? They were all there. There were ten or maybe fifteen of those murderers. They stood in a semicircle, with their machine guns across their chests. What difference does it make which one? They all gave orders, they all shot! All of them!

PROSECUTOR: Please calm yourself. I am terribly sorry that I have to provoke you with such questions. But you see, we can only convict people if we can *prove* that they committed murder. You say that all the members of the local Gestapo were there. But it could be that one of them was on leave, or possibly on duty in the *Dienststelle*. And didn't shoot.

FIRST WOMAN: Every one of them shot. If not that day, then another. During the second or third action, during the liquidation.

PROSECUTOR: The law requires proof. And I, as the prosecuting attorney, am asking you for proof. I am asking for the names of the murderers, the names of the victims, the circumstances in which they were murdered. Otherwise, I can do nothing.

FIRST WOMAN: (*quietly*) My God . . .

PROSECUTOR: Excuse me?

FIRST WOMAN: Nothing, nothing.

PROSECUTOR: Please think: which one of them was in charge of the selection in the square?

FIRST WOMAN: They all participated in the selection. Kiper, Bendke, Hamm, Rosse. They were standing in a semicircle.

PROSECUTOR: Standing? Were all of them standing? Or perhaps some of them were seated?

FIRST WOMAN: No, they were standing. Is it that important?

PROSECUTOR: It's very important. Do you remember seeing a table in the marketplace at which several Gestapo men were seated? The others were standing near the table.

FIRST WOMAN: A table? I don't remember. There was no table there.

SECOND MAN: Here's the map. The marketplace was shaped like a trapezoid. At the top was the town hall, a beautiful old building that had been built by a Polish nobleman in the seventeenth century. The jewel of the town. The square sloped down towards the actual market where the stores were, as if the town hall reigned over the place. On the left, by the ruins of the old ramparts, stood those whose *Arbeitskarten* were taken away and also those who did not have *Arbeitskarten*. Note that the streets radiate out like a star. Here's Rozana, then Sienkiewicza, then Piekna, then Male Targi, then Nadrzeczna. There was no river in the town, but maybe once upon a time there was one, and that's why it was called Nadrzeczna—Riverside. Then came Zamkowa Street. All the streets I've named were later included in the ghetto, with the exception of Piekna. Beyond Male Targi there was a cemetery. Yes. That's where they were shot. Nadrzeczna was adjacent to the cemetery. Most of the people who lived on Nadrzeczna were Poles, but it was incorporated into the ghetto nonetheless, because of the cemetery. Because the cemetery played a major role in our life then. Between Rozana and Sienkiewicza there were shops. First, Weidel's pharmacy—he was killed in the camp; then Rosenzweig's iron shop—he was shot during the second action. Then Kreitz's dry goods store, the Haubers' restaurant and hotel—they were the wealthiest people among us, their daughter lives in Canada—and then two groceries, one beside the other, Blumenthal's and Hochwald's. They were rivals all their lives, and now they're lying in the same grave. Oh yes, I can draw every single stone for you, describe every single person. Do you know how many of us survived?

PROSECUTOR: Forty.

SECOND MAN: How do you know?

PROSECUTOR: They are my witnesses.

SECOND MAN: And have you found all of them? And taken their testimony?

PROSECUTOR: I have found almost all of them, but I still haven't taken testimony from everyone. Several witnesses live in America; they will be questioned by our consular officials, and if necessary, subpoenaed for the trial. Two live in Australia, one in Venezuela. Now I would like to ask you about the details of the selection that took place during the first action. When was it, do you remember?

SECOND MAN: Of course. It was a Sunday, in December, towards the end of the month. It was a sunny, cold day. Nature, you see, was also against us. She was mocking us. Yes, indeed. If it had rained, or if there had been a storm, who knows, perhaps they wouldn't have kept shooting from morning till night. Darkness was already falling when they led those people to the cemetery. Oh, you want proof, don't you? The snow on the town's streets was red. Red! Does that satisfy you?

PROSECUTOR: Unfortunately, Mr. Zachwacki, snow doesn't constitute proof for judges, especially snow that melted twenty-five years ago.

SECOND MAN: The snow was red. Bloody Sunday. Four hundred fifty corpses on the streets. That's not proof? Then go there and dig up the mass graves.

PROSECUTOR: I'm interested in the selection. Who was in charge of it?

SECOND MAN: Kiper. A thug, a murderer. The worst sort. I can't talk about this calmly. No. Do you mind if I smoke? These are things . . . I'm sixty, my blood pressure shoots right up. A cutthroat like that . . .

PROSECUTOR: How do you know that Kiper was in charge of the selection?

SECOND MAN: What do you mean, how? I gave him my *Arbeitskarte* myself. He peered at me from under his brows and snarled, *"Rechts!"* I went to the right. Saved. Saved until the next time.

PROSECUTOR: Please describe the scene in more detail.

SECOND MAN: I was standing some distance away. We all tried to stand as far away from them as possible, as if that could have helped. I was standing near the Haubers' hotel. It was one in the afternoon. The church bell struck one, and since it was quiet in the square, you could hear the bell clearly even though the church was in a different part of town, near Waly Ksiazece. By then they had been calling out names for about an hour. Suddenly I hear, "Zachwacki!"

PROSECUTOR: Who called your name?

SECOND MAN: One of the Gestapo, but I don't know which one.

PROSECUTOR: Didn't you notice which of them was holding the list?

SECOND MAN: No, you're asking too much. There was a list, because they read the names from a list, but I didn't see it. If a person saw a scene like that in the theater, maybe he could describe it in detail. This here, that there, and so on. But when a tragedy like this is being played in real life? You expect me to look at a list when my life is hanging by a thread? I was standing there with my wife. She had an *Arbeitskarte* from the sawmill—that was a good place to work—and I had one from the cement works. Also a good place. When they called my name, my wife grabbed my arm. "Let's stay together!" she cried. Dr. Gluck was standing nearby, a kind old doctor. He told my wife, "Mrs. Zachwacki, calm down, your husband has a good *Arbeitskarte*, you have a good *Arbeitskarte*, get a grip on yourself." But she kept saying, "I want to stay together, if we don't we won't see each other ever again. Albert," she said, "I'm afraid." I literally had to tear myself away, she was holding on to me so tight. There, you see, so much for instinct, intuition . . . I never saw her again. All the women who worked in the sawmill were sent to the left. (*he clears his throat*)

PROSECUTOR: (*a short pause*) Then what happened?

SECOND MAN: I dashed through the crowd. There was an empty space between us and them, you had to walk about thirty meters to cross the empty square. First—I remember this—someone kicked me, who I don't know. I took a deep breath and ran as hard as I could to get to the town hall as fast as possible. When I handed them my *Arbeitskarte* my hand was trembling like an aspen leaf, although I'm not a coward. Not at all!

PROSECUTOR: To whom did you hand your *Arbeitskarte*?

SECOND MAN: I already told you, to Kiper. He opened it, read it, handed it back to me and snarled, *"Rechts!"* I was young, tall, strong. He gave me a reprieve.

PROSECUTOR: At the moment that you handed him your *Arbeitskarte*, was Kiper standing or sitting?

SECOND MAN: He was standing with his legs apart, his machine gun across his chest. His face was swollen, red.

PROSECUTOR: And the rest of the Gestapo?

SECOND MAN: I didn't see. I don't remember if any of them were standing next to Kiper.

PROSECUTOR: Did you see a table?

SECOND MAN: Yes, there was a table, but it was further to the right, as if it had nothing to do with what was happening there.

PROSECUTOR: A small table?

SECOND MAN: No, not at all. It was a big, long oak table, like one of those trestle tables you see in monasteries. It was probably one of those antique tables from the old town hall.

PROSECUTOR: Long, you say. What were its dimensions, more or less?

SECOND MAN: How should I know? Two, three meters. The Gestapo sat in a row on one side of the table; and there was quite a large group of them sitting there. Bondke was sitting, Rossel was sitting—them I remember. And there were at least six others.

PROSECUTOR: Did you by any chance notice whether Kiper was sitting at the table earlier and whether the reviewing of the *Arbeitskarten* took place at the table?

SECOND MAN: I didn't notice. When I was called, Kiper was standing several meters from the table.

PROSECUTOR: Who do you think was in charge of the action?

SECOND MAN: Kuntze. He had the highest rank.

PROSECUTOR: Did you see him in the square?

SECOND MAN: I don't remember if I saw Kuntze. Presumably he was sitting at the table. But I only remember Bondke and Rossel.

PROSECUTOR: Was the table already there when you got to the square?

SECOND MAN: Yes.

PROSECUTOR: Who was seated at it?

SECOND MAN: No one.

PROSECUTOR: Some people claim that Kiper was sitting in a chair even before the table was brought out and that afterwards he sat at the head of the table. That he took the *Arbeitskarten* while he was sitting.

SECOND MAN: It's possible. Everything is possible. When I was called, Kiper was standing.

PROSECUTOR: Mr. Zachwacki, do you recall an incident with a mother and child who were shot in the square?

SECOND MAN: Yes, I do. It was Rosa Rubinstein and her daughter Ala. They were from another town and had lived in our town only since the beginning of the war. I knew them.

PROSECUTOR: Who shot them, and under what circumstances?

SECOND MAN: I was standing in the group of workers on the right side of the square, beside the well.

PROSECUTOR: Please indicate the place on the map. With a circle or a cross. Thank you. There was a well there, you say. No one has yet mentioned that well.

SECOND MAN: It was an old well, wooden, with a wooden fence around it. All around it, in a semicircle, there were trees, poplars. At one moment I heard a shot, and people who were standing somewhat closer said that Rosa Rubinstein and her daughter had been shot. It seems that both of them had been sent to the left, but they went to the right. People said that Kiper ran after them and shot them.

PROSECUTOR: You said, "I heard a shot." Do you mean you heard a single shot?

SECOND MAN: Those were my words, but it's hard for me to say if I heard one shot, or two, or three. No doubt he fired at least twice.

PROSECUTOR: Did you see the shooting with your own eyes?

SECOND MAN: No. I saw the bodies lying on the ground. They were lying next to each other. Then the *Ordnungsdienst* picked them up. A red stain was left on the snow.

PROSECUTOR: You were part of the group that helped to bury the victims afterwards?

SECOND MAN: That's correct. There were so many victims that the *Ordnungsdienst* had to take twenty men to help. Four hundred and fifty people were killed in the town—in the square and in the house searches—and eight hundred and forty were shot in the cemetery. My wife was one of them.

PROSECUTOR: (*pause*) But you didn't see any murders with your own eyes? Can you say, "I saw with my own eyes that this one or that one shot so-and-so or so-and-so?"

SECOND MAN: I saw thirteen hundred victims. The mass grave was thirty meters long, three meters wide, five meters deep.

SECOND WOMAN: No, I wasn't in the square. Because I worked as a cleaning woman for the Gestapo, and in the morning, when everyone was going to the marketplace, Mama said to me, "See if they'll let you stay at work." I took my pail and a rag and a brush and said goodbye to my parents on the corner of Mickiewicza and Rozana. We lived on Mickiewicza Street. My parents kept going straight, and I turned onto Rozana. I had gone a few steps when suddenly I caught sight of Rossel and Hamke; they were walking towards me and I got terribly frightened, so I ran into the first gate, and they passed by, they didn't notice me. Later I saw them entering the building at number 13. I kept going.

PROSECUTOR: Who lived in the house?

SECOND WOMAN: I don't know, I was young, I was thirteen years old, but I said I was sixteen because children, you know, were killed. I was well developed, so I said I was

1 6 1

sixteen and they let me work for them. That was good luck. That day the Gestapo were going around to all the houses looking for people who hadn't gone to the square, and if they found someone, they shot him either in his apartment or on the street.

PROSECUTOR: Was there a family named Weintal in the house at number 13?

SECOND WOMAN: Weintal? No, I never heard of anyone with that name. I stayed at the Gestapo all day long, hiding. I knew the building, I knew where I could hide. Well, I must say, I certainly was lucky.

PROSECUTOR: Which Gestapo members were in the building that day?

SECOND WOMAN: I don't know. I was hiding in an alcove next to the stairway to the cellar, at the very end of the corridor. Once I thought I heard Wittelmann's voice; he seemed to be on the telephone and was yelling something awful.

PROSECUTOR: Did you ever witness an execution while you worked there?

SECOND WOMAN: I know that they took place, and I know where. But I never saw them shoot anyone. I was afraid, and as soon as they brought someone in, I would hide, get out of their way. I was afraid that they might shoot me, too. They killed them against the fence.

PROSECUTOR: Which fence?

SECOND WOMAN: There was a courtyard at the back surrounded by a fence, and behind the fence there was a trench. That's where they were shot. I know, because afterwards the *Ordnungsdienst* would come and collect the bodies. Once I saw them carrying a doctor whom they had killed. His name was Gluck. But that was after the first action, in the spring. Another time I saw a group of Gestapo men walk out into the courtyard and immediately afterwards I heard a burst of machine-gun fire.

PROSECUTOR: Who did you see then?

SECOND WOMAN: Bondke, Rossel, Hamke, and Wittelmann.

PROSECUTOR: All together?

SECOND WOMAN: Yes. All together. I was washing the stairs to the cellar then.

PROSECUTOR: Were they all armed? Did each of them have a weapon?

SECOND WOMAN: Yes.

PROSECUTOR: Those shots you heard then, were they from a single machine gun or from several?

SECOND WOMAN: I don't know. I didn't pay attention. I wasn't thinking that someday someone would ask me about that. Maybe one of them shot, maybe two. Maybe they took turns. How should I know?

PROSECUTOR: When was that?

SECOND WOMAN: That was even before the first action, probably in the fall.

PROSECUTOR: Do you know how many people were shot then? Do you know their names?

SECOND WOMAN: I don't. I didn't see their bodies being taken away. I saw them collect the dead only once or twice. I don't know who was killed then.

PROSECUTOR: And you never saw a Gestapo man fire a gun?

SECOND WOMAN: No. I only worked there until the second action. I couldn't stand it any longer, I preferred to go to a camp. In general they were nice to me and never did anything bad. Once Bondke gave me cigarettes. The best-mannered was Kiper. He was an educated man, like Kuntze. But the others, no. Kiper had a lot of books in his room. He wanted fresh flowers in a vase every day. Once, when I didn't bring flowers, he yelled at me. Once he broke the vase because the flowers were wilted. On the desk in his room was a photograph of an elegant woman with a dog. But it was Hamke who had a dog. I used to prepare food for the dog. His name was Roosevelt. A wolfhound, very well trained. He tore the druggist Weidel's child to pieces. I heard Hamke boasting about him: *"Roosevelt hat heute ein Jüdlein zum Frühstück bekommen"*—Roosevelt had a little Jew for breakfast today. He said that to Kiper, and Kiper screwed up his face in disgust. Kiper couldn't stand Hamke and used to quarrel with Bondke. In general, he kept to himself. He didn't drink. That Sunday he was the first to come back from the marketplace.

PROSECUTOR: How do you know it was Kiper? Did you see him?

SECOND WOMAN: I heard his voice.

PROSECUTOR: Who was he talking to?

SECOND WOMAN: He was talking to himself. I thought he was reciting a poem. Anyway, that's what it sounded like. Then he went to his room and played his violin—I forgot to say that he was a trained musician. Bondke used to make fun of him and call him *Gestapogeiger*—Gestapo-fiddler. I don't know much about music, but I think he played very well. I heard him play several times. Always the same thing. I don't know what melody it was, I don't know much about music.

PROSECUTOR: Did you see him that day?

SECOND WOMAN: No, I only heard him playing.

PROSECUTOR: What time would that have been?

SECOND WOMAN: I don't know. It was growing dark.

PROSECUTOR: Could you hear the shots from the cemetery inside the Gestapo building?

SECOND WOMAN: I don't know. Maybe not. The cemetery is on Male Targi, and the Gestapo headquarters was on St. Jerzy Square. That's quite a distance. But maybe in the silence, in the clear air . . .

PROSECUTOR: Did you hear any shots when Kiper returned?

SECOND WOMAN: I can't say. Because the way I felt that Sunday and for several days afterwards, I was hearing shots all the time, and my parents thought I had lost my mind. I kept saying, "Listen, they're shooting . . . ," and I'd run and hide. Mama took me to Gluck, who gave me a powder, but it didn't help. I kept on hearing shots for a week. It was my nerves.

PROSECUTOR: When did the other Gestapo men come back?

SECOND WOMAN: I don't know. When it got dark, I sneaked out through the courtyard and returned home. The city was empty, as if no one was left alive. I was astonished: the snow was black. That was the blood. The most blood was on Sienkiewicza Street, and on Rozana. I didn't meet anyone in the marketplace either. It was empty. In the center of the square, lying on its back with its legs in the air, was a small, broken table.

Jewish Lives

IDA FINK
A Scrap of Time and Other Stories

LISA FITTKO
Solidarity and Treason: Resistance and Exile, 1933–1940

RICHARD GLAZAR
Trap with a Green Fence: Survival in Treblinka

ARNOŠT LUSTIG
Children of the Holocaust